DARK
CONSTELLATIONS

Also by the author
Savage Theories

DARK
CONSTELLATIONS

POLA OLOIXARAC

TRANSLATED FROM THE SPANISH BY ROY KESEY

SOHO

First English translation published in 2019 by
Soho Press
853 Broadway
New York, NY 10003

Library of Congress Cataloging-in-Publication Data

Oloixarac, Pola, author. | Kesey, Roy, translator.
Dark constellations / Pola Oloixarac ; translated from the Spanish by Roy Kesey.
Other titles: Constelaciones oscuras. English

ISBN 978-1-61695-923-4
eISBN 978-1-61695-924-1

1. Scientists—Fiction. I . Title
PQ7798.425.L65 C6613 2019   863'.7—dc23   2018057680

Interior design by Janine Agro, Soho Press, Inc.

Printed in the United States of America

10 9 8 7 6 5 4 3 2 1

for EK

Hic captabis frigus opacum.
—Stendhal, 1829

Hacking is not a spectator sport.
—Erik Bloodaxe, 1995

DARK
CONSTELLATIONS

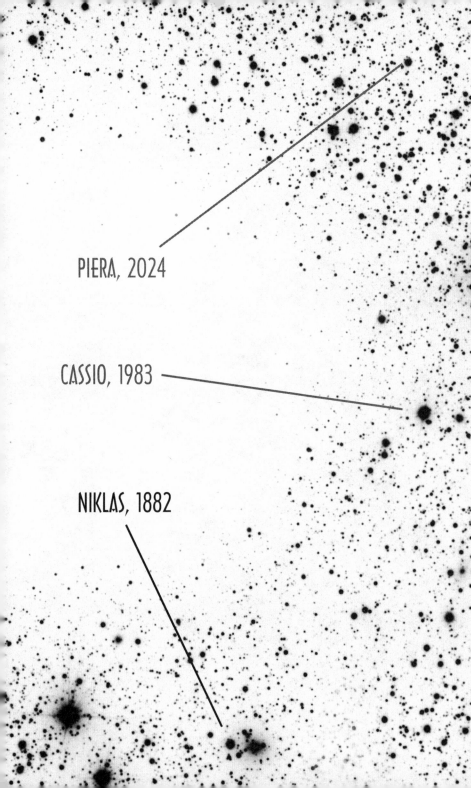

PIERA, 2024

CASSIO, 1983

NIKLAS, 1882

On the final day of 1882, a group of explorers reached the sea that surrounds the crater of Famara, the volcanic mass that rises up from the archipelago of Juba. Like a fortress on the water, the crater's aerial line shrouded the bay in grandeur. The travelers made land on a beach of black sand scored by the tails of lizards, and began their climb along a mossy trail through a series of gorges that wound their way through the sinuous formations of dark lava. Anchored in the bay, their ship looked like an old dinosaur, its viscera extracted by parasites who lowered the cages, bronze instruments, wooden traps, and coils of rope into the sand amidst the boulders onshore.

The explorers advanced into the cold, humid scrub growing beneath trees that intertwined high above; from time to time the sky opened in a gleam of white. They walked for hours toward the valleys of the island's interior, across an expanse void of human trace. The island, though submerged in the sand-specked mist that came from the Sahara, was thick with *Crissia pallida*, the spidery green flowers with nuclei of gold pollen whose extraordinary properties would remain all but unknown until the beginning of the twenty-first century.

The story of these visitors is woven into the belief system of the Guanche religion of Mahan. It is said that as night fell, the foreigners entered the island's deep valleys, still guided by what they took for faint stars, but what they thought was the vault of the sky had become the roof of a cave thick with insects. (They would later swear they'd seen the inverted face

3

of Auriga, the constellation over Orion, blurred by the mist.) As a result of this misperception, Zacharias Loyd, the captain of the expedition, didn't give the order to stop for rest until, all but dead, they'd finally reached mineral soil; it later horrified him to think that no one, not even he himself, had noticed anything strange about the clamor made throughout the cave by devils who would only show their true nature once the throat-like passageway had led the explorers to a subterranean lake.

At this point, Niklas Bruun, the youngest member of the expedition, knelt to sketch what he could see: the insect merchant Diotimus Redbach, holding a lepidoptera the size of his hand (*Noctilia pubescens*). The shadowed profile of Marius Ballatinus, orchid hunter. Two other men, hunched down over the water, their backs to the artist; they must be Pavel Ulrich, a zoologist of shadowy acclaim, and Captain Loyd, who was tracing measurements in the air, estimating the cavern's dimensions. The explorers will report "luminous creatures gliding along the surface of the water," though Niklas Bruun, in particular, will leave room for doubt, as his eyes were "agitated by the touch of darkness." In the sketch, Pavel is skimming the water with his fingertips, his gaze lost in the cavern's depths. And in the darkest corner is a man who can only be Torben Schats, then at the pinnacle of his fame as a cartographer of vanished islands. He is touching the rock walls in calm veneration, and the cave hollows out above him, an ovaloid arch of stalactites enclosing the scene.

4

Arriving at the highest point within the crater, still
without having slept, the explorers came upon a series
of disturbing monuments. They will compare them to
disfigured sphinxes, though they admit they'd never
seen anything like them before. These seemingly human
forms were only an introduction to a monstrous repeti-
tion; one of the monuments is composed of eight human
feet attached to a head that appears to be resting, its
eyes closed. Niklas Bruun draws them covered in dried
algae, with blue and gray shadowing that he reserved
for apparitions at the bottom of the sea.

Here the explorers began to make sense of the labyrinth of caves that exists beneath the island's surface,
the system of subterranean grottos that snakes about
below the crater floor: the sea flicks its tongue underground, the water coursing through chutes into caverns
dozens of kilometers long, which must have been given
form by huge bubbles of air and gas created as the lava
flowed down in a cloak of smoke and chaos from high
in the sky, plunging finally into the sea. According to
the history of the Guanche sect, the members of the
expedition (to whom must be added Suri-Man, Betú,
and Sasha, the slaves) passed through a valley of scalded
rock and arrived at the hidden village of Mahan, but
as they wandered amongst the deserted monuments,
exhaustion overcame them, and they lay down to sleep,
a single great snoring beast made of men, one on top
of the other. In the sky, birds circled.

They were awakened by the murmuring crowd.

Time to make a pact with the natives. Calm and cheerful, the local inhabitants ("bare torsos, pudenda covered with sheep-skin garments") led them through a maze of grottos to a large round cavern in which the most distant stalagmites looked like a group of expectant creatures, softly gilded by some special light. Far above, a hole in the rock opened to the sky.

The sun is so strong outside that it would leave the travelers blind, so they concentrate on capturing the cavern's internal flora—the burnished lichens and blue anemones are home to albino turtles, crabs, and other crustaceans whose meat is transparent—and put off collecting specimens from the surface until the following day. At night, the chanting begins, the dancing and the drums; Bruun describes a group of natives who meander about, talking with their eyes rolled back. They enter into a colloquy with their gods, and from behind the stalagmites appear several dozen local women whom the explorers hadn't seen before. Meanwhile, Venus advances ardently, cutting across the sphere of the sun; in the course of this phenomenon, which occurs twice a century, and to which wonders and catastrophes are often subsequently attributed, the gravitational pull of Venus drives animals and ocean tides mad, uniting the silent, brutal forces of the earth and sky. From the surface of the island, however, one can barely see through the opaque haze that comes from the Sahara and spreads itself across the archipelago. And now the visitors began to commingle with the natives, entering into the genetic history of the island in a torrent of semen and blood.

* * *

The commentators have estimated that there were approximately twenty-three girls, as well as a handful of adults with shell-hard skin, that took part in these ceremonies on this island, where trees can live for several thousand years (*Dracaena draco*, vegetal dragons whose dry skeletons branch into cartilaginous crests, and which contain a dark lymph famed for its regenerative qualities). The members of the expedition believed they were suddenly part of an astonishing fertility ritual; as the orgies begin, the descriptions lose their habitual precision. In a timid but denotative style marked by periods of discomfort, the young Niklas Bruun describes the women advancing individually or "in groups of two or three," throwing themselves with a tranquil ferocity onto the explorers' genital geysers, twisting down over the tips of their organs.

Though the light shed by these documents is dim, it allows the reader to follow a number of concurrent events. Each female takes in each foreign organ several times, with an average yield of three milliliters of seminal fluid per act; after each contact, the men fall into a profound state of torpor from which they do not emerge until another woman arrives. The men describe how, hypnotized, they saw pearlescent opals in the darkness—annelids that fell from high above, spinning in the air, luminous. In Bruun's illustrations, "the ladies of the island" appear spread like spiders over the bodies of the travelers; he establishes that the women "conceded minimal refractory periods," until the semen was followed by water, then by fine threads of blood accompanied by pain and urea.

Incapable of resisting, the men allowed themselves to be devoured by the darkness of the grottos for days on end.

In another set of documents, Niklas Bruun describes the sight of the island of Juba ascending in a column of flame from the bottom of the sea, a volcano rising from the depths in a maelstrom of power and speed; the sea commingles with the sky, the fleeing tide exposing a barrier reef, the trapped fish and seaweed drying into skeletons that the haze engulfs. The image of the lava merging with the sea vapors was captured in a series of exceptional drawings: the slow fiery river advances, consuming the earth on a night perfumed with sulfur. Bruun also describes a ritual meal of white butterflies (*Lycaenidea poppa*): soft-bodied, with a faint taste of coconut milk, they are decapitated against one's palate in one quick motion, and their bodies are sucked dry; he adds a minuscule elegy to their high protein value, noting that they are his main food source for the duration of his stay on the island.

* * *

The *Daily Telegraph* is the first to report on Bruun's journey. The paper must be deliberately courting controversy with all of its conflicting accounts: it packages the narrative as a perverse variation on high-seas romance, and then runs alongside that the testimony of natives contacted by a mysterious Guanche who resides in London. The Guanche contentions are as emphatic as they are contradictory:

1. That the Guanches never lived on that part of the island, which was reserved for the demonic denizens of the volcano.
2. That given how jealously protective the Guanche culture is of its women—it is forbidden to speak to a woman alone in the countryside unless she speaks first—the tale told by the explorers must have been born of Guanche boasting about the magical powers of their tribe; the white butterflies that inhabit the grottos are in fact a Guanche delicacy, and the Guanche people, who had already turned back the French and the Spanish (this time, of course, the invaders traveled under the flag of science) would have administered near-lethal doses in order to preserve their liberty.
3. That on the other hand, not a single specimen collected alive ever made it off the island, and it wasn't even clear what the voyagers were doing there.
4. That the "ladies of the island" never existed.

5. That the ladies of the island saved the semen of foreigners in their bodily reservoirs so as to later discharge it stealthily into bowls, that the village survived for months by cooking up these human juices, and that the incursion coincided with the peak of the insect mating season.

Of the men who entered the crater and swarmed zealously around the holes offered by the native women—whether said holes had been drilled by force or as the result of a fascination so persistent that it seemed mutual—the young naturalist Niklas Bruun reached immortality the soonest. His memories of what took place across the ocean during the Transit of Venus circulated, mutating, as they were passed through the sensationalist press of the era. By the time news of his adventures on the Famara expedition reached the most erudite botanical circles, young Bruun was already a celebrity.

His drawings were published to great success at the height of the scandal; as noted by Vernetius Lodi, a rival botanist turned involuntary biographer, "the society pages made little effort to hold themselves back at a banquet table packed with candid proof that the cream of scientific aristocracy was embroiled in a strange coital affair." Though it left their reputations in ruins, the matter imbued the travelers (slowly, like bronzes waiting for the heat that will temper them) with a certain heroic glow. But until the Royal Horticultural Society mounted its exhibition of exotic plants, few had noticed.

Niklas, at seventeen years of age, smiles absently in a photograph; a few meters away, women are watching him, hair adorned with dried scorpions. He had a sort of darkly romantic European look. His velvet clothes could hardly keep women from seeing through to his true raiments: they pictured him surrounded by giant serpents hanging down from skeletal trees, stalked by jaguars and cohorts of primitive beings on the verge of slaughtering him, enwrapped in a jungle aura that not even these elegant salons of iron and glass could dissipate. On the day of the exhibition, he is depicted with his latest acquisition in his boutonnière: *Psychopsis papilio*, an amulet signaling his alliance with a sweetly terrifying caste. As for whatever it was that surrounded him like a cloud of latent remoras from some strange and mysterious world, it was assumed to be related to the youngster's mark of distinction: his sexual initiation in the Famara crater.

All this portended the birth of a golden monster in the competitive world of botany, one who had his eyes on the legendary heights which the discipline had been claiming for some time; for Niklas, any other profession was unthinkable. He was privy to aspects of the private lives of insects that mapped perfectly to his own. Meanwhile, the effects of *Crissia pallida*, which could overthrow opiate derivates in the illegal dreams of humankind, stayed secret.

Between the ages of seventeen and twenty, Niklas Bruun set down in writing his *De Flora Subterranea*: the vivid, elliptical, and at times frankly incomprehensible book that foresaw the apocalyptic trajectory of the Anthropocene. What others described as a possibility, he actually saw in hallucinations. His notes chart cave systems that plunge hundreds of kilometers out into the black Atlantic, home to whole kingdoms of beings unknown to science.

The early descriptions didn't merely record instances of strange rapport between plants and insects. They tell of secret pacts between species, in locations beyond human reach. Niklas's writings bore witness to a series of soundless but violent transformations, "slight but fundamental changes" that had arisen, dark patches distributed en masse among humans and nonhumans alike, on a spatiotemporal scale that rendered them invisible to the eyes of men.

Surfacing at a time when various naturalist theories offered competing descriptions of the world, the phenomena recorded by Niklas Bruun in the course of his research trips give an account of the moment when species separated into two groups to conquer both land and sea. There were baffling outcomes, floating far from the galaxies where the essential questions were being defined, but until they were added to the catalog of Anthropocene disasters, even "Anomalies" seemed too tame a label. Later on, Bruun's discoveries would be retraced, and his very body would become part of the

Humans and Hybrids Collection.[1] It would not be clear until far later that the phenomena incorporated a matrix of forms; this fact would become one of the cornerstones of the Project.

This is the only surviving photograph of the research team formed by Max Lambard and Cassio Liberman Brandão da Silva at the dawn of the Project, when they first began their work on Stromatoliton. It was taken in 2016 or thereabouts, when the first syntheses were verified. The image shows an early prototype of what would later be a cadaver laid out for dissection. Cassio, in glasses, is seated with one hand slightly raised, like someone speaking up in a medieval painting; Max Lambard's hands hold two of the cables from one of the very first prototypes. There are no known photos of Max's face from when he was alive.

At the moment in question, the men were faced with a codex of data still unwritten, the trance of a theodicy, a philosophy composed of the sum of their acts. This is their story.

---

1 We have his brain. The Project acquired the specimen from a biobank; its structure contains new elements of considerable interest.

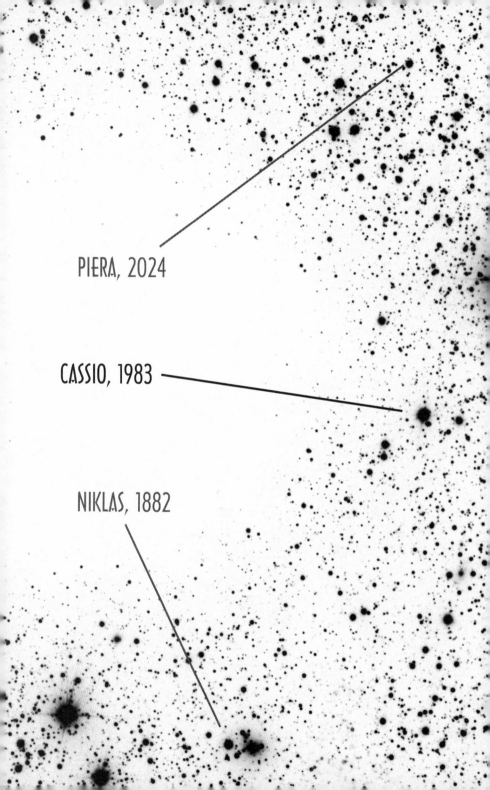

PIERA, 2024

CASSIO, 1983

NIKLAS, 1882

assio's first steps in the world of the capitalism involved a solitary, poetic use of computational tools, with occasional forays into their overall destruction. When his mother lifted him up so that he could leave globs of saliva on human faces, little Cassio shut his eyes. The fat baby's gestural repertoire didn't yet include smiling; at times he puckered his lips, but wasn't able to conclude the grin successfully. He was a serious child. His chestnut hair fell in a curtain around his ball-shaped head; his chubby cheeks belied the wary distance he kept from the world.

In the summer of 1983 one of the largest mass mortality events ever registered in equatorial waters took place on the island of Fernando de Noronha, Brazil. The penguins had ridden a cold-water current and swum hundreds of miles north before approaching the white sands of Noronha, only to die in the suffocating heat. The daily newspaper *Estadão* carried on undeterred: a face-off between local gangs had resulted in ten deaths; a storm of breathtaking size was drawing near; people were advised not to leave their homes.

For several days, Sonia had noticed masses of ants wandering her white furniture, forming ovals that later disappeared; it was now clear that they were coming from the ceiling. The mother (Sonia) deposited her son (Cassio) in his high chair and adjusted the straps. At first he wouldn't stop howling, but after eating he entered the state of drowsy wellbeing that is particularly pronounced in future fat kids. Coffee in hand, Sonia drew near to the invisible nest; the ants were enormous, muscular, so the path of the invasion (though not, perhaps, the relentlessly increasing size of the colony) was easy to ascertain.

Sonia put her mouth up to a crack in the wall and blew; ants fell into her mug and spasmed in the acidic bath.

A biographical sketch of the molecules that would end up composing young Cassio—the prelude to his expert hacker phase in the age of anarchic capitalism—must begin at another latitude. The beaker holding his DNA was located in Porto Alegre, capital of the state of Rio Grande do Sul, Brazil. Recalibrating the image, one can see Sonia Liberman, the blonde daughter of a prosperous Argentinian real estate agent, in a supine position, wearing a very short flowery dress, receiving violent bursts of seminal discharge.

The trajectory in question found Sonia propelled across the Argentinian-Brazilian border as part of her university's labor force in 1981. The head of social anthropology at University of Buenos Aires, Juan Carlos Carrales, had interviewed her in the hope that she would join his research team, which was traveling to Brazil for fieldwork. Her hard work and excellent grades were duly noted, and after a few meetings Sonia (who was actually a linguistics student, and had never done fieldwork in her life) received her letter of acceptance: two months in Porto Alegre and its neighboring villages researching modes of coexistence between Kaingáng villagers of the Jê linguistic family and the *fazendeiros* that descended from Indian hunters.

Sonia was the only woman in the group. There were two other advanced undergrads like her, Mauricio and Pío, and two graduate students, Gustavo Levas and "El Teto" Rattachi. She knew Mauricio and Pío from her anthropology courses; her interactions with them had been agreeable, almost friendly.

Sonia and Gustavo shared the eighteen-hour bus ride to Porto Alegre, during which he threw himself into descriptions of his experiences as a missionary in Somalia, his plans to make a name for himself in fieldwork with indigenous peoples, his fluency in Quechua and São Paulo–accented Portuguese, and everything else he could think of that might impress her.

In the early eighties, Porto Alegre was the gilded cradle of Brazilian livestock. Away to the south from the turmoil of Rio and the sluggishness of the northeast, with ample land and a temperate climate, the region had positioned itself as Brazil's moral reserve. It was in Porto Alegre that the Workers Party (PT) was born, and it was the *gaúcha* elite that propelled the PT onto the national stage. A product of miscegenation between Trotskyite elements, theologians, and ex-*guerrilleros*, the PT would end up working with the Argentinian government to promote the DNA mapping initiative, known as the LatAm Genetic Data Unification Project. But none of this could yet be spotted on the horizon in March of 1981, when the institutions of both Argentina and Brazil were under military control, and collaboration between university institutes was still rare.

Brazilians were more direct than Argentinians. Early on, Sonia looked favorably upon the Brazilian tendency to hold hands, to look one another in the eye: the collective instinct to touch one another and laugh together. Brazilians gave two kisses to say hello, and goodbyes included a hug, occasionally with an extra bit of fondling at the waist; in general their friendliness seemed genuine, as if it truly gave them pleasure to make your acquaintance.

On her second day there, the head of the Brazilian group, Luíz Fábio Fondas, invited the Argentinians to a friendship dinner with their local counterparts. Charming and soft-spoken, Luíz Fábio guided Sonia off to one side of the restaurant, his arm sliding around her waist, fluid as a snake in water.

He wanted to introduce Sonia to his wife, Maria da Graça Maibrán Schutz, a striking blonde, her maw painted pink, triangles of green plastic in her earlobes. Maria da Graça opened into ample hugs (*Prazer em conhecê-la!*), amassing Sonia in a turmoil of lipstick and curly hair. After a couple caipirinhas, Sonia's research colleagues suddenly seemed mysteriously intelligent, as if they had unraveled the secrets of contemporary life, sharing them privately amongst themselves. It also seemed to her that all of the men now had an extra expression at their disposal, indicating, perhaps, that they belonged to the primate council dedicated to the lowliest of the species' activities.

Surrounded by their youngest viziers at the head of the table, Luíz Fábio and Carrales exchanged the ritual gestures of chief anthropologists. It was indisputable that Levi-Strauss had infused the discipline with extraordinary oomph here in Brazil, at a time when educated Argentines only appeared capable of dreaming up scansions of Marxist dogma; measured against the sum of upper primate history on Earth, it was no big deal, but at least, reasoned Carrales, it was something. He spoke with restrained solemnity as he took hold of a bottle of soda water and let the liquid gush slowly, the others listening calmly but intently.

The presence of Maria da Graça was a show of local strength, but the Argentines had their own blonde—Sonia, younger and single—so it wasn't yet clear who had the upper hand. Unaware as to the table's geopolitics, Sonia toyed with her serving of *abacaxi*. Her throat was a little sore, giving her a tendency to roll her tongue back toward her palate. Maybe it hurt because she'd been mixing guttural and nasal sounds, she thought; speaking competent Portuguese required tightening one's perineum and ululating from one's lower belly, movements to which she was unaccustomed. A bit lightheaded from the *cachaça*, Sonia excused herself and went to get some air.

Outside, a flagstone path carried out into a grove of palms. There was a wooden arrow painted green, and Sonia followed it. She walked among the immense fronds that had fallen from the trees and laid stretched out like octopi. To her side, the magnificent Lagoa dos Patos shone brightly beneath the gigantic moon; the aroma of the night was intensely vegetal. The stars of the Milky Way could be seen gathering, dense and violet against the black velvet. She sensed that someone was following her, but didn't see anyone.

The path led her to a hut covered with plants and vines where the *banheiros* were hidden. Inside, Sonia leaned down over to dampen the nape of her neck; in the mirror she saw that her hair was disheveled, her cheeks flushed from the alcohol and the heat. She never saw his face. He came up slowly from behind. Spinning her around, he stuck his tongue in her mouth, pressing her firmly against the tap. Responding to what she suspected to be an exercise in local custom, she curved her body slowly backward, attempting to avoid the kiss, to send a message of doubt, reserve, femininity. In spite of this nucleus of coyness, her movements propelled her pubis against him.

Their tongues entwined slowly, reptilian, not a word passed between them. Sonia confirmed the intimate, nearly suppli-cant form of his erection; when he began to caress her thigh, extending his hand so as to trace with one finger the edge of the tanga she had acquired that afternoon in a shop on Rua da Praia, Sonia took courage, and detached her mouth to take a breath. She asked him if he was a member of the research team. Smiling, her unidentified *beijador* asked what part of Argentina she was from.

The sexual exchanges propagated in Brazil en masse during temperature peaks would later be charted in tidal waves of DNA data, sweeping through digital leviathans; at the time, however, Sonia's situation felt like a private event, closed and sufficient unto itself, with only the two of them taking part, a love affair. Extracting herself from between the twin pipes of the tap, she whispered, "Buenos Aires," a bit discomfited in the face of his confidence. She left the bathroom with smudged makeup, her mouth swollen by his kisses.

In Tupinambá mythology, encounters between different species are considered part of a magical realm. One species begins by imitating another, adopting the other's movements in order to eat them, but their love story exceeds the arc of humanity. Upon its own death, the eater species awaits a reencounter in another world so as to devour the other species again. Sonia walked close along the handrail, admiring her own intrepidity; her heels undulated, almost liquid.

In the sky, the moon shone iridescent, while in the lower kingdom of men, the owners of the restaurant had put music on, and separated the tables a bit so that people could dance. The Brazilians shook their arms and hips to the rhythm; the Argentinians clomped about as best they could. The song playing was the "Disco Samba" medley by the Belgian pop group Two Man Sound—all the rage during the 1982 World Cup.

Caipirinha in hand, Gustavo stood apart from the dancing and watched. Now that he had arrived in Brazil to fulfill his destiny, he had no intention of wasting time in the conga line of university politics; he preferred getting wasted. He saw Sonia come in out of nowhere and sit down alone at a table, searching for something in her purse. He came up slowly from behind, and spoke directly to the nape of her neck:

"You don't dance?"

Startled, Sonia turned her head without losing control of the lipstick at her lips. Gustavo leaned in close:

"I mean, given that we've crossed the fortieth parallel, we should embrace their primitive behavior, if only in the name of mimesis."

Sonia ran her hand through her hair and dropped her gaze; she hadn't liked his comment. Gustavo was perfectly familiar with the feminine code: fixing the hair and lowering the gaze were parts of a symptom cluster that would give him the chance to rub his protuberances against hers until he could eventually insert himself, triumphant. He sat down beside her, smelled her arm. She seemed a little drunk; it was only a matter of waiting. From the black speakers came Rita Lee singing her 1979 hit "Chega Mais":

I know that face
I know that voice, that smell
That crazy look
That fire, that thing
Scandalous, you are gluttonous
And you want to kindnap me

A shadow set a cold beer on the corner of the table. "Excuse me, but I don't believe we've been introduced."

Gustavo watched the new arrival through the round edge of his caipirinha glass. That the girl he liked should be stolen by a Brazilian mapped perfectly to one of the shared prejudices that unify the continent geologically. A product of Ibero-African blends, Brazilian masculinity contained so many mutated genes that it had room for both the ugliest and the most exalted elements of the race; the affront was, to Gustavo, an unstoppable phase in genetic-historical materialisms the sort of destiny that left his own sex appeal down among the bland and unattractive, and who knows, maybe Chileans. He refused to battle and faded into the background, returned to the bar, ordered a whisky. Sonia was still touching her hair. *Then you take me home . . . You torture me with kisses . . . Until you make me confess . . .*

Sonia wasn't used to being easy. Now, naked and horizontal, she took João Fernando Brandão da Silva to be the missing link to *sapiens sapiens*. She learned that, beyond his dark thighs, his well-turned body, and that majestic lance enveloped in blue veins, João Fernando was a successful aeronautical engineer.

He didn't have anything to do with her university research team, had in fact been sitting at the next table over, but he swore that from the moment he saw her walk in, he hadn't been able to take his eyes off of her. He worked for Varig, the aviation company, and was here at the invitation of their local office; he told her that this was his last night in Porto Alegre. His next destination was São José dos Campos—"*You should come visit one day*," he said with a smile.

She let herself be penetrated in the missionary position, and after that, in spite of her initial protests, from behind; she choked violently during fellatio, and he consoled her by kissing her passionately. Sonia then experienced what subsequent pornography consecrated as a "Brazilian bang," popularized by the televised orgies of the Carnavals in the Complexo do Alemão; completely doubled up beneath his hands, she could barely breathe. João Fernando hadn't been with an Argentinian before, but appeared to have certain ideas; in the postcoital chat, he once again murmured that her attitude, in general, was very Argentinian. "But I've never met a girl like you," he said in solid Spanish, which Sonia shattered with kisses.

That night they went down to the beach; back in the restaurant overlooking the Lagoa, the research teams inhabited a far-off, illuminated fish tank. In the sky there was a meteor shower, and João Fernando took her by the hand, the flickers of light crackling in his retinas. Her body seemed lighter than before, the sweat at her temples curled her hair, the night pawed at her through the flowery dress. Sonia felt happy. On another order of certitude, she had encountered the source of DNA that she would strive to reproduce.

Cassio's progenitors consolidated their new relationship by lying together at night in the soft sand of Canasvieiras, one of the top resorts in the early 1980s. Theirs was the type of relationship that wasn't destined to last, one wherein the exchange—the suppuration—of sexual fluids serves as core. João Fernando soon left his job at Varig, lured away by Embraer, which was to become the leading manufacturer of commercial aircraft in Latin America.

The Brazilian Embraer began in the Argentine province of Córdoba, after World War II. It was Kurt Tank, a refugee from the Third Reich, who laid the foundation for the first viable airplane built on South American soil, the Pulqui II. Under the alias Pedro Matthies, accompanied by a group of fellow Germans who had hidden their brown shirts safely away to escape to South America, Tank designed a plane intended to be the *dernier cri* in jet aircraft. Under his tutelage, the Aerotechnical Institute became the Military Aircraft Factory, and there he built the South American successor to the Messerschmitt, an evolved version of the Luftwaffe mainstay, albeit influenced by the admiration and anxiety that Soviet engineering had provoked: that is, a synthesis of the best craft of its era.

Argentina had been the last nation to withdraw its support for the Third Reich; unlike Brazil, who had bet on the Allies and, as a show of allegiance to the United States, established internment camps on Brazilian soil for Japanese immigrants, Argentina was all in on Nazis right to the end. The year 1945 found Argentina on the side of evil, while Brazil consolidated its diplomatic love affair with the United States, the new global police; for Argentina, that was the kickoff of decline. The year 1945 is deemed by many the beginning of the Anthropocene era, when nuclear weapons foreshortened our sense of the earth; however, Argentina's links with the Nazis allowed her to import the fleeing German brainpower, which resulted in the largest technological investment in regional history. A explosion in slow motion, the Anschluss had greater impact in the Americas than any previous attempt of industrial dissemination.

Many of the scientists who'd fled the Reich ended up with no choice but to park their top-flight engineering brains in minor industries, like the manufacture of home appliances and water heaters. Soon, the cycle of Argentine political instability set in motion by the Anthropocene caused substantial losses within Kurt Tank's hand-picked staff. Many of the brains that carried his engineering virus didn't hesitate to move abroad in search of better conditions; Brazil capitalized on this diaspora. Unlike Argentina, Brazil decided to shut down the effort of building a military air fleet and focus on commercial aircraft. The country began to attract new waves of scientists into its matrix of influence, eventually drawing in luminaries of nuclear and particle physics such as Richard Feynman, who became famous throughout the cabarets of Rio de Janeiro for scribbling equations on napkins during striptease shows. The Embraer fleet, now competing evenly with Boeing, is the direct descendant of this first infestation of German cerebral capital in Brazil.

Political crises punctuated further diasporas from Tank's institution, even as Argentina maintained its role as an engineering training ground. In fact, João Fernando had learned his lilting Spanish by reading Argentinian aeronautics manuals—a feature that he shared with the president of his country, Fernando Henrique Cardoso. Among Kurt Tank's men was one Ronald Richter, who would transport his hydrogen bomb project to a small island a thousand kilometers south of Córdoba (Bariloche, 1948) in the first South American attempt to become a nuclear power.

According to Professor Carrales, Brazilian industry was blessed to have developed behind the back of high culture. "It integrated itself into the bourgeois capitalist paradigm without ever passing through the domestic and domesticating sphere of culture, with a capital *C*," he explained, spreading his arms. His shirt was open down to his solar plexus; a thin gold chain shone beneath his Adam's apple. Sonia remembered her first interview with Carrales quite well: his glass of Scotch, his dark tobacco cigarettes. A cigarette began its voyage from the ashtray to his mouth as he once more jumped ahead to the conclusion:

"The Brazilians have just started climbing down from the palm trees; millions of them are still up there, but when they all come down, they're going to take over and God help us all then."

He assured Sonia that the research project had the support of the departmental leadership, so there would be sufficient funding to guarantee continuity. He might also propose a new project involving cultural anthropology, a field on the rise:

"For example, the mating rituals of each region—what is

vulgarly known as pornography. You see it in American porn films: the female takes control of her own penetration, using the formula, 'Fuck me, fuck me!' She's giving an order, is clearly pressuring the male, is expecting a high-quality performance, and the male responds to her demand. Now, what happens in South American cultural products of this type? The female emits messages like, 'Oh, no, no, are you really going to do that to me? Oh, please, no . . .' The verbal begging is set *in contrast* to the body language of the female, which demands—that is to say, orchestrates—the act of copulation. There is probably a regional evolutionary advantage involved in our need to alleviate as much as possible the weight that the male must bear in the course of his performance, our determination to allow him to be the one applying the pressure rather than suffering it. Which brings to mind the invention of syphilis here on South American soil. It was one of our first export products based on a European component, in the sense that at the beginning, the colonists feared or were disgusted by the natives and preferred to have sexual contact with llamas and sheep instead. Which is to say that as a zoonosis, syphilis is a product of the horror that the colonists felt at this circumstance of total control over the one penetrated, at the shift from pressured to pressurer. That switch from the passive participle to the *-ens* form of the present participle is hardly a trivial matter—you took Latin, right?"

In sum, there was a great deal to do, and Carrales proposed that they get together for coffee more often. After she met João Fernando, however, Sonia dodged messages from Carrales for weeks, and finally sent him a letter of resignation.

João Fernando took her to live with him in São José dos Campos, in the state of São Paulo. The leading companies in the air and space industry were settled there; the couple made their home in one of the most exclusive *jardims* of São José, where the engineering elite of Embraer, the Institute of Aeronautics, and the National Institute for Space Research all lived. The beach, a paradise lined with coconut palms, was two hours away by car. Eager to adapt to her new ecosystem, Sonia hired an architect to help decorate her spacious apartment in the eco-minimalist *"fazendeiro urbano"* style that was all the rage. She learned to cook Bahiana meals, and put *dendê* oil in everything. It had been Sonia's independent ways that threw her into this immeasurable country in the first place; she soon saw her life reduced to sexual encounters with her husband, nightly dinners, and *café da manhà*.

Her social life consisted of outings with the "Embraer wives," the spouses of her husband's colleagues. These gatherings took place in magnificent apartments stacked in graceless concrete cubes with ample covered parking. São José was a very ugly city; the newest buildings were covered with tile, like the interior of a massive bathroom open for all to see. Sonia would have preferred to live in a house with a yard, to take personal ownership of the feral promise of a life in Brazil, but she too had to get used to living indoors. At the time, the Brazilian bourgeoisie on the rise was still a small, endangered creature, a species that had to be nourished and protected in paddocks surrounded by electric fences and watched over by armed doormen. In spite of herself, Sonia quickly adopted the notion that she formed part of a threatened white minority, a professional ghetto still in its cradle, surrounded by savages; though São José was two hours away from the city of São Paulo, the state as a whole was a violent, dangerous place. When she and her husband visited friends—all high-ranking engineers at Embraer—Sonia stayed tight up against his back as they entered, letting drop a timid and sulky *"Olà, tudo bem?"*

She later realized that these friends didn't expect anything special from her—that love was simply understood in Brazil, was in fact taken for granted, much as everyone assumed in Argentina that Sonia's husband would never abandon the basic principles of life as a male in exchange for quiet intervals of pussy-whipped pleasure. The idea of starting a family that was completely her own, one where she could invent her own rules of discipline and adoration, fueled Sonia's sexual marathons. Sex was much more interesting when the risk of procreation was real.

João Fernando's job became more and more demanding, with constant trips to São Paulo and the Embraer offices in New York. Alone in her spotless apartment, Sonia gave herself over to nostalgia for her childhood in Argentina. She listened to the music of El Nano Serrat, María Martha Serra Lima y Los Panchos, and the magnum opus of Julio Iglesias (*El Amor*, 1975) on cassettes that she rewound with ballpoint pens, returning again and again to "Mi Dulce Señor" and "Algo Contigo."

Though she did everything she could to block them out,

she couldn't always keep her thoughts from returning to scenes from the jungle. The disgusting taste of those strange orchids (she'd only tried the *labelli*) and the weeks of fever, the friendliness of the natives, which made everything seem aberrant and fake, the boredom she felt among the Indians, the trips out to collect those fleshy plants, Rattachi's shouts in the middle of the night, and the tense evenings spent watching the Jê watch them, thinking that the natives had poisoned them and were calmly observing the results of their dark magic. And after that, nothing. She couldn't remember anything, except one memory filtering through the others: images of day inside images of night.

One morning she'd woken with rope marks on her hands. Her head ached; her bed was stained with sweat and strewn with loose grass and soil. She was completely exhausted, as if the night had kidnapped her, carried her away to the fever's center, and the fever itself had rubbed grass all over her. She could barely stand. She stuck her head outside of the tent and saw a group of rats disappear under a bush; farther away, the natives were cooking something, and laughing. In this world, she remembered, the deities came together to feast in celebration of each death. To be, to exist, is to walk about between two worlds in a half-devoured body; stalked on both sides by death, there was no way to escape.

Sonia never filled out her research reports. She also avoided going back to Argentina, and gave the university no explanation; her files and fieldwork were eventually added to a folder labeled "Nonexistent." Within her immediate human perimeter, the women began reproducing so as to give their husbands what they desired: little engineers with whom to build Embraer Mini model airplanes and visit their respective soccer tribes (Corinthians, Santos, and São Paulo were the most popular teams). Sonia's trip to Brazil had coincided with her first professional experience, the grand opening of a world based on intellectual training, but she had chosen another path without hesitation—one spent in the apartment wearing lingerie, madly biting João Fernando's ear, whispering that she loved feeling his pole in all its splendor, piercing her vulva *ao natural*. When the research team's two months were up, they returned to Buenos Aires without her.

The trip had completely transformed her, she knew it. She never learned what had occurred during those weeks in which her mind went dark, had no interest in reading anyone's reports. Gustavo had tried to see her one last time, but only managed to get ahold of her by phone. He'd insisted: she was abandoning her research career! But appealing to her ego via her profession was very much the wrong approach.

She slides across the surface of the water, a blue dart in the blackness. The water iridescent. The world below in silence, estranged from the sky.

The foam comes in waves, covers the meadows of violet seaweed. The sea stretches out above the sky, hides the black creatures. Far away, the horizon glows lime green.

A sound sends a shudder through her body; blows of incandescent light come from within. She trembles, moves faster and faster. She feels drawn to the tunnels' dark holes. The fearsome abyss ends in an undulating cave of fresh black water in which to shelter, its shape reminiscent of a skull.

There are others awaiting the signal as well.

It's said that the Yacana make their way through the waters of a river. It is truly a very large river. It comes from the sky, becomes blacker and blacker. It has two eyes and a very long neck. It comes walking down from the sky covered in mud.

They'd never been described. The human gaze had never fallen upon them. The LatAm project harbors these beings inside.

In the afternoon, Sonia changed Cassio's diaper and called a taxi. She hadn't seen her husband in two weeks; all she knew was that he was on a trip to the New York office. She made her way down to the landing, her hand guiding the stroller jangling with gold bracelets. She wasn't sure they'd let her take the child out of the country without the father's written consent, but she was determined to try. The driver got everything loaded in; water poured down the tiled walls of São José. A grayish fog descended over the valley. The child started to cry.

At the airport in Guarulhos, she went up to the line of pay phones. When she managed to get through to Embraer New York, a feminine voice informed her that Mr. Brandão da Silva was in a meeting; she called back, and the voice said that he'd just stepped out. Sonia hung up. Her long eyelashes panned across the noisy airport; in the line for customs, a man insulted two women in uniform, attracting the attention of a few others, curious and bored. Abstracted from the world of men, little Cassio slept peacefully in his stroller.

As she boarded the airplane, Sonia allowed an elegant executive from Rosario to carry her coat. She was still a beautiful woman with fine, delicate features; while waiting to board, several men had been monitoring her movements. At the baggage claim, the executive from Rosario came over to wish her a pleasant stay and give her his card; she could call him if she needed anything, in Buenos Aires or anywhere else. Sonia extended her neck, let him kiss her on the cheek.

There would always be loves in her life—there was nothing to fear. Her father was there in the Ezeiza airport to pick her up; he hugged her with tears in his eyes.

That night, an underwater cloud of jellyfish crossed the formidable mud banks of Río de la Plata. This whirlpool of tentacles entered the viscous depths of the port of Buenos Aires in a display of destructive potential hidden beneath a lightning storm.

Many moons since she last went to the surface. Iridescence and scale, she bites at her own immobility. The lime green light climbs up toward the stones that bow before her. She can breathe, exist within herself, can fall toward the abyss she holds deeper still. A carapace begins to form inside her.

She impregnates herself with parts others have left behind, her scales growing ever harder. When she emerges—if she ever does—she will be much stronger. She doesn't yet know what form she'll take.

She has come from a river that is too warm, ever warmer, came in search of cool black water. She once watched a subterranean continent travel slowly far into the air, then bury itself entire in the caves.

She awaits the signal. The thunderclap comes soon enough, the distant light flashes across the sky, unites with the lymph, feels itself explode.

Science was not yet prepared for such cadavers.

efore his genetic trajectory began to delineate itself like a laser—before the fringe activities that would catapult him to underworld glory amongst the primeval hacker groups—Cassio revealed himself to be a really good kid. He was interested in the things of the world; he liked reading newspapers, liked *Página 12*. He was fat, soft, and pale, and he was capable of detecting the pain of others, and once he had localized it, was able to show interest in ameliorating it. The phase of enjoying control over other living beings wouldn't manifest itself until much later.

Every afternoon his grandfather would take him to the botanical garden in Palermo: small shady green hills, zig-zagging trails, and old greenhouses of iron and glass. The Botanico was the green space closest to his house, and home to the largest community of cats in all of Buenos Aires. When Cassio learned that the felines had adopted the area as their permanent residence, that they were in fact *his neighbors*, the thought fascinated him to the point of stupefaction. He watched them cavorting in the sun, chasing one another around or simply depositing themselves like pastry buns in the grass; at times he threw himself down in the gravel and extended his fat little fingers toward them. The cats watched him impassively, or fled, leaping like rabbits.

He wasn't sure how it all began, didn't know how his mind had begun to fill with thoughts of nocturnal patrols, couldn't trace the origins of the mysterious process by which his mind had penetrated the darkness for the very first time. But a few blocks from his house, the reverse of the city was undergoing spasms of malignant behavior. Cats young and old were stuffed in bags and loaded into trucks, which took them to unknown locations, quagmires beyond the reach of law and morality. The police reports couldn't confirm the whispered rumors: that the cats were taken all the way out to the Warnes shelter, thrown onto the heap of trash at the bottom of an empty elevator shaft. Gasoline and human cruelty did the rest.

It was later learned that the Warnes shelter had been demolished to make room for a Walmart. But the story of the kidnapping and disappearance of felines had made its way from the mouths of doormen and old ladies to the vegetable stands and newspaper kiosks, where the children were infected; the image of the kittens mewing desperately, scratching out one another's eyes as they tried to escape, sent Cassio into action. He took a ream of white paper and a thick marker; on each page he wrote NO TO THE FELINE HOLOCAUST and added a drawing of Toulouse, Marie, and Berlioz, the main vectors of tenderness in *The Aristocats* (Disney, 1970). He pasted the posters up on the walls of his school, the prestigious Scholem Aleichem, and quickly organized a protest amongst his little classmates.

The principal couldn't comprehend the redemptive nucleus that moved Cassio and his henchmen to action, and threatened them with suspension for making jokes about the Shoah. The young protestors didn't balk; their sobs and screams were explosive missiles directed at the adult nervous system, and they began a sit-in "of indeterminate duration" to commemorate the dead animals. It was Cassio's idea to make cat silhouettes, drawing profiles on the school patio like the chalk outlines of murder victims. Without realizing it, he had both deduced and put into practice one of the most resoundingly effective PR strategies of the Mothers and Grandmothers of the Plaza de Mayo, a movement that protested the government-run kidnapping of children under military rule previous to the country's return to democracy. The chalk cats filled the patio in a variety of colors.

To calm him down, Sonia gave Cassio an actual kitten. It was a tabby, with yellow and orange tones morphing subtly into black stripes. From a distance it was a bit of a redhead, like Cassio himself, who baptized it with the name of Axl Rose. He quickly indoctrinated it in the concepts of goodness and mercy; in the language of *felis catus*, these are rendered as steady purring and conscientious licking.

However inadvertently, Cassio was moving counter to the instincts of other children his age, wherein ferocity walks hand in hand with the discovery of hatred and physical strength. Terrified hamsters dangled out over balconies and gerbils saddled with firecrackers are of course often the first witnesses to youthful experimentation with fury. Crouched in the swimming pool at the KDT club, where Sonia had sent him to learn how to swim, Cassio watched kids playing Submarine—the larger children attempting to drown the smaller ones.

He had read about aliens who came to Earth to be born among humans, anonymous beings inoculated against the drama of mankind. Some of this had been confirmed by Donatello, the Ninja Turtle with the purple mask. Donatello was the engineering genius among Cassio's favorite chelonians, adoptive sons of Splinter, an extremely intelligent mutant rat who had learned the techniques of his ninjitsu master—his beloved human—and returned to live among his own kind. The secret of the turtles' mutations made them part of an enlightened, shadowy caste, but in one terrible episode, Splinter, who had taught them both science and combat, was forced to submerge into the depths in search of Donatello. Hypnotized by the evil enemy, Donatello rejected him, calling him, most painfully, a *rodent*. Born rebels, the Ninja Turtles and their leader lived happily in the sewer system until their mission was finally made clear, and they at last *made contact with the world above.*

Back then, Cassio was experiencing his own precocious submersion: he had discovered the Viking and Voyager space missions, whose photos and documentation he obtained by writing letters to NASA. His missives were simple but heartfelt, scribbled and rescribbled until he'd managed a legible draft—his handwriting was deeply deformed. The 1990s phase of the Clinton Pax Americana had not yet begun, and the Reagan administration spared no expense creating propaganda to foment the cosmic anti-Communist dreams of children all over the world. The reports arrived in a language that he didn't understand very well, so he focused on the mission photographs, which could have been taken straight out of *Cosmos*, *Contact*, and *Comet*, the three burnished masterpieces of his hero, Carl Sagan. His constant companion, little Axl, served as a feline Buddha amongst the posters of outer space.

Several years later, onstage to receive top honors at the Interscholastic Mathematics Competition, Cassio would stammer through a remembrance of his furry companion, who was always *between* one thing and another, licking himself or simply incarnating a form of intermittence; Schrödinger demonstrated that he'd understood something important about felines when he decided to involve them in his illustration of quantum physics. If Cassio focused on his memories of the prize ceremony, he could see it all again—everything streaming down at him, the anxious parents and bespectacled teachers, boxes of croissants and clusters of children, each entity fitted into its spatiotemporal slot—and was once again certain he'd been surrounded by robots. This feeling had solid foundations: he'd also begun to sense the presence of spectacularly sordid powers nesting in his very being, a sensation his instinctual prudence counseled him to keep secret.

His mother hadn't let him take Axl Rose along to the school, and poor Axl, whose reproductive apparatus had already been rendered inoperable, got used to a life of stalking scraps of paper and peeing on the plants on the balcony of their neighbor in 5B, and he got away with it for a couple years, until the cat was fatally poisoned. He spent the final hours in agony beneath an armchair, and that's where Cassio found him, already stiff. The wake Cassio held consisted of *Appetite for Destruction* played at top volume: for three days the music was audible five floors down and out into the street, but not even those songs at that volume could hide the thunder of his sobs.

Cold phrases descended from the adults around him, geysers of tar streaming from their mouths, gestures that signaled nothing but condescendence in the face of death. Something of his relationship with the world, of his confidence in the human race, was lost forever. How had no one yet hacked the problems of evil and death? And why should one respect the present order if its leaders hadn't even noticed these problems—of if they had, were incapable of solving them?

Young Cassio's existential urgencies did not lead him to a love of lyrical theology. They did not place him at the center of the universe, equipped with anguish and voice. They did not turn him into an orphan of becursed lineage, nor did they land him on a densely overgrown islet in the turbid shadow of a *personality*; strictly speaking, his new powers didn't require that he engage in any particular behavior. The same urgencies that could have turned Cassio into another young Werther merely left him at a certain cognitive distance from other people, an armored eye with which to observe the world. The human sphere, much like the feline one, was full of suffering and pain that flowed down from the sky in black waves, awaiting the right moment to drown him.

An illness hastened the distancing process. His cheeks became gaunt and yellow, and his eyes sunk in their sockets, their lids tinted violet. Cassio couldn't remember exactly how the information he needed had reached him; he knew television had no part in it. It felt like it had always been part of him.

Sonia panicked at the sight of that shadow beneath her son's eyes. At the time, Gustavo Levas was staying at their house, which made her all the more sensitive to memories of the trip to Brazil; she still had nightmares about the horrible rashes on Rattachi's body when it was brought in. Cassio detected her moment of vulnerability, and rapidly executed the command, making clear that "no" was not among the viable responses. Sonia obeyed immediately, and little Cassio finally had the desired package, one whose enchanted geometry he had conjured up during the early fevers brought on by Koch's bacillus.

His IBM XT came with two joysticks, 128 kilobytes of memory, and a DOS reference manual. His incursions into Wolfenstein constituted his first soundings of the depths of immortality. With the manual's help, he learned to alter the machine's internal parameters, designing ploys that would multiply his lives within the game and create super-powerful bombs. He played with fierce seriousness. Somewhat later he would begin exploring the world of juvenile delinquency, in perilous numeric adventures where he would meet his future henchmen and business partners: Jony and Mat, Luck and his doppelganger Wari. By the time Cassio was fourteen, he had written a program that exploited a vulnerability at the National Bank, and had impassively, even disdainfully, confronted several nation states and their laws. He'd hijacked computers at the Pentagon, and taken control of various local networks in Argentina and Brazil. The university's engineering department and the newspaper *Clarín* had the most powerful servers, so he made them his slaves, having come to the realization that the illnesses of living systems created perfect opportunities to penetrate them.

n the early months of 1993, Cassio managed to assimilate a few features of masculinity that had previously eluded him. His body stretched out a bit, promoting him from chubby to "big-boned"; he committed to heavy use of pine-scented cologne. He walked around with a skateboarding cap on backward, which attenuated the explosion of thick curly hair. Dead Kennedys T-shirts floated about his body until they disintegrated, with pride of place going to "Too Drunk to Fuck" and "California Über Alles." He was partial to Pink Floyd and the Beastie Boys, and spent his afternoons watching MTV Latino, wherein a long-haired Mexican guy introduced different varieties of metal to the pimply audience sitting in the dark.

Traces of his mother remained in the products he used—the semiotic smell of anti-lice shampoo still flaring around him. But his mind was too busy with more fundamental issues to dedicate itself to cutting every namby-pamby element out of his life. He considered getting a Smurf-blue tattoo of Satan (a synthesis of his opinions about the lie of religion), but the soft feel of his pale, slightly flabby flesh inspired a feeling of self-compassion. By this point, his research had become clandestine.

He gained access to the knowledge that would change his life just before his hormones began to overwhelm him. Data flowed over him, tidal surges of information and wonder. Back then, the internet was still an archipelago of small isolated groups, elite excrescences growing around

BBS servers, staring out at the ocean that would soon flood their existence.

Cassio wandered alone through the estuaries of unknown file extensions and reports on alien beings, of conspiracy theories (back when the magnitude of evil was still in doubt), and, most valuable of all, of tutorials showing how to hack ever more complex systems. It wasn't easy to gain access to the Satanic Brain BBS, the Mecca for larval hackers like him. Neophytes had to prove their worth, negotiate hostility and a series of tests, cross through a forest strewn with sharpened stakes and deep black holes, before they were allowed to learn the secrets of the armory.

The introductory screen informs him that he has to work his way through a question tree in order to enter. After several attempts, he reaches a screen that reads, YOU ARE WITH VIRUS. Cassio jumps up, turns off his computer. He waits a few minutes, then connects again.

Hello? he types. The word VIRUS blinks, an underscore next to it like the protruding foot of an animal in hiding.

Hello appears in tiny letters. Cassio gasps. He has just found his way into Satanic Brain; Virus is a person, and potentially a friend.

He would later learn that Satanic Brain was run from the shadows by Azeta, then an adolescent just a few years older than him. When they finally met at a bar in Almagro, AZ didn't stop talking. He told Cassio that one of his archenemies in the *viri* world, Fubu, had coined the phrase, "A wounded virus is a wounded animal," and had managed to spread it throughout the civilian world, where it had appeared in several print media outlets. The phrase obsessed AZ, and appeared to infuriate him. "A virus is an animal that never dies!" he said, pure mystic certainty. He set his Coke down and looked over; Cassio took a sip of his own through a straw and nodded.

That night, Cassio got a message: *Your face reminds me of Walter, my new lizard embryo. See you around.* AZ lived with his mom and played his evil-computer-kid role extremely well. The arc of his life, of his journey of self-discovery, was just beginning to define itself; it would later lead him to cover his body with tattoos and fill it with food.

Even before learning that AZ collected embryonic lizards, that Luck could phreak with nothing but his voice, mimicking the melody of electronic pulses to avoid paying for telephone calls, that Mat controlled several satellites, which he used to hack other satellites, so as to create a dark fleet in the sky— that is, before his new friends revealed their wondrous true forms—Cassio was witness to another series of revelations, those of beings whose nature as humans he wouldn't have been able to confirm.

In pornographic films, the climax of each individual scene consists of the money shot; eventually the scenes converge in the narrative climax of the orgy, the cephalopods built of human flesh. A series of monstrous transformations ensued, and attention shifted from hole to hole, creating groups of beings that were progressively more complex, whereby a single surface covered unseen interior spaces. Double and triple penetration of the female was a common theme, multiple aggregations into tense muscular cumulous clouds. Cassio sometimes shot the magma of his being into the nearest

Coke can, gathering these remains of himself. The human cephalopods confirmed a deep intuition: that everything could be penetrated, opened, *rebuilt in the purest of terms*—terms native to a machine whose form was still foreign to him, but that he, advancing obsessively step by step through his environment, would eventually come to know and control.

The little predator had been born within him. This wasn't the first time he'd felt it move.

The next few years—the new moon of his training, preparation for his first mission—saw his fascination with the machine solidify. He was a firsthand witness of one of his era's key periods: the birth and reproduction of early computer languages, specific and porous, variegating like species of plants. He studied low-level programming in C and Assembler, and thus drew closer to the machine, to its most intimate commands, with one objective: to learn how to take advantage of the flaws and vulnerabilities that would allow a hypothetical attacker (and, to the extent it was possible, a *real* one) to turn an automobile, or any other apparatus capable of receiving signals, into an explosive device.

In the year 2020, as part of the team that built the software for Stromatoliton at the dawn of the LatAm Genetic Data Unification Project, Cassio would remember with fondness these embryonic hours of his professional career. In interviews he gave about the Project, he speaks of the childlike eagerness that persists in his research, uniting each successive phase of his mind into a precise, concise staircase. A certain air of innocence remains in his chubby, as yet unaltered face, and daily pimples only smoothen the crests of his megalomania.

His reading at the time consists of Gibson and Lem, but he mentions *The Little Prince* as a favorite for its two crucial lessons: a) that what is essential cannot be seen from the surface (because we can only find the vulnerabilities in software by submerging ourselves in it), and b) a boa truly could swallow an elephant (because anything is possible). Then he shrinks back, and his chin trembles a little; a burst of weakness reveals the child of yesterday (his allergies acting up as he breathes in a bit of mildew) in the scientist of today. The interviewer asks again about how he got started. Transported by early memories, his pride returns.

Even back at the beginning, he knew that he had the technical gifts to achieve frightening levels of mastery, but he was missing the most essential thing: a nickname, a personal banner. This was no trivial matter. It put him face-to-face with transcendental questions. Should his handle provoke terror (Satan666, Chucky) or wisdom (Obi-wan, Yoda)? Should it be something private and cryptic (asdfgh) or a cultural marker (bladerunner, hobbit)? He wasn't a unicorn or a centaur or even an elf; what he had in common with these beings was that he didn't really exist either.

One day Sonia rushed into his room, a human cyclone. Some men were at the door asking for him. Cassio couldn't find his glasses, observed the men through fog.

He was being accused of penetrating the computer systems of the Botanic Garden branch of the Bank of Boston. Sonia was furious. But when the men realized that a twelve-year-old kid had made a mockery of their system's defenses, their primary reaction was embarrassment. In exchange for a report on weaknesses in the bank's network, the matter would be dropped; when they invited him to use their servers on the condition that he help them patch their domains, young Cassio Liberman Brandão da Silva chewed down on his smile of victory. His hobby had become an asset. Sonia, however, had other plans.

Cassio couldn't just spend all day at the computer, she decided; Saturday classes at the School for Little Inventors couldn't be his only time out of the house. Malevolent and prescient, she coordinated logistics with Susy Waskam, a neighbor there in the building.

Prodded along by their mothers, the irritated boys emerged into the outside light. His head covered with dark tufts of hair, Leni had the physical aplomb of Kermit the Frog's first cousin, and like that character, he preferred a certain sartorial seriousness—polo shirts and glasses that gave him a gravitas rarely found in *Anura neobatrachia*. He and Cassio had run into each other several times in the building's elevator, and both had shared harrowing rides with the albino twins from 7C. Cassio never looked directly at them; he merely watched them in the elevator mirror, which hardly softened the ferocity of their psychotic gaze. Leni lived on the eighth floor. Manuel, his hamster, had once fallen onto the twins' balcony. They had an iguana, and had let him touch it: Leni slid his hand along the scaly body of Joaquín, who kept his eyes closed for as long as the contact lasted. The heroic hamster, meanwhile, had not only survived the adventure but opened the door to the lair of the albinos, who, like Leni and Cassio, lived with their single mother, no permanent male adult in sight.

Leni sidled up to Cassio and spoke slowly to him: they were clearly still too young, he said, for creatures of the feminine sex to be throwing themselves at them, begging to be penetrated. It just wasn't going to happen. He didn't mean to be overly blunt, but, just in case Cassio hadn't ever considered the question, he had to ask: What was the point of going to the club? There just wasn't any reason, concluded Leni. He'd been studying the matter.

Cassio looked at the subtly scaly skin of his new friend. He checked his Star Wars Swatch and looked at the sky; it was lewd with light, heavy with heat. It was nine A.M., the workday barely begun in the world of men. Leni was right. But the time would come.

This same bus would drop them off at home at six P.M., the end of the workday for children. Cassio and Leni sat up front; every so often their meatworms stiffened in alert, smelling the possibility of spread buttocks. Then Mora appeared.

Mora Baum: whatever it was that she secreted, it intoxicated the girls as well. She had chestnut hair and eyes that ranged from nebulous Neptune to a phosphorescent green (specifically, that of the algae that sometimes floated offshore, visible from the Costanera—a rare lime green that people said was brought on by the biological experiments that were taking place on the Martín García Island, a few hundred miles from Buenos Aires). She lived in the Luis María Campos y José Hernández Tower, climbed onto and off of the bus followed by a comet tail composed of variations of herself, little crowds of girls that Cassio couldn't tell apart. Sometimes she wore a crown of flowers, and other days she dressed entirely in pink; a genuine alpha female, Mora was venerated and feared by her followers. Even the idiotic *madrijs*, the club's chaperones, were accomplices to her halo of impunity; they looked the other way during the treasure hunts, pretending not to see Mora and her friends systematically spying on those who were hiding the treasure.

With Mora leading the way, the girls had colluded to induce Judith Gugelkorn's brother to admit something under duress: *The only thing boys want is to stick it in.* The girls weren't stupid, had already realized this, and Mora made the doctrine her own, forcing him to download the charts of the natural law of sex right there in front of her little friends.

For most of that summer, the little masculine elements at the Hacoaj Country Club were condemned to wander in circles in the desert of disaffection just like their Mosaic ancestors thousands of years before. While "Caca" Heller and their other enemies tended to gang together and cuss, thereby highlighting their most unpleasant features, Cassio and Leni decided to ignore the girls completely. They would never honor a hierarchy based on petulance, unratified by any sort of logic. To prove this, one day Cassio penetrated the herd of girls and invited Mora Baum herself out for ice cream. To the stunned surprise of her friends and the idiot *madrijim*, Mora accepted.

And it was Mora herself who, under the willows of Hacoaj, took hands-on interest in the contents of Cassio's trousers. She looked at him steadily as she slid her hand down, the movement a bit brusque, which made him jump. With her other hand she took off his glasses, and then she kissed him, her lips softly parted. Cassio unclenched his fists and reached out; something in her responded to his touch like an alert reptile. He put his glasses back on, and concentrated on

Mora's bra, on the goose bumps that spread beneath her blue Hacoaj sweater.

The feeling that she had recognized his true self glowing like a golden beast in the dark jungle, that everything else was a parody for the benefit of noninitiates—those incapable of reading the true code behind the aggressive payload— produced a devotion so strong that for a time he oscillated far from the deconstructed computers and logical fields that were his natural habitat. He was enthralled by the lilac light that pulsed from Mora's body, his little divine supernova. Every so often he allowed himself to collapse into a chair beside Leni for a quick Wolfenstein tussle, but the deadly reality of the game was only a copy of a copy; he only became fully absorbed at the end of each match, gripping his joystick tightly.

In the mornings, the bus gently rocks the surreptitious erection that writhes like a worm in his pants. Would he run into Mora? Would he feel her candied touch? Perversely, the club's summer session ends when school begins. Cassio decides to take the bull by the horns.

He lifts the lamb's-wool collar of his jean jacket, combs his hair straight back. The mighty tower rises at the corner of La Pampa and Luis María Campos, the tinted glass crests of its roofline slashing at the sky. The glazed door slides open. The security guard is watching a soccer match on a tiny screen; focused on his destiny, Cassio ascends in the mirrored cube. The elevator's metallic plates open onto a luminous carpet. There are two lions painted gold. Diana stands erect between them, likewise beautiful, bearer of the chromosomic secret of his beloved.

"Morita, you've got a little friend here to see you," she calls.

She winks at Cassio, and he clenches his teeth.

"Come in through here. It's the room just past the mirror."

Cassio lets himself be led along the blond carpet. The lavender furniture makes the room glow pink. On a small bookshelf there is a row of My Little Ponys. "Hi," he says, and unsheathes his portable chessboard.

Mora watches him advance into her territory; her kissable little mouth is closed. She sits down straddle-legged on the rug and opens the chessboard, examines it. Cassio sits down across from her. His gaze traverses her doll-like freckles, her eyelashes fluttering in the vanilla-scented mist. He says that if she doesn't know how to play, he can teach her.

Mora informs him that she knows perfectly well how to play. Her father taught her—he's a DAIA delegate, so they're always playing chess. Her little skirt forms a gazebo over the organelles that, in Cassio's imagination, are smiling in his direction.

Within a few minutes, Mora has lost a knight and her queen. Her T-shirt sags open, revealing smooth little hills, little puddings of orange and strawberry. Cassio breathes in their aroma, squints, proposes starting a new game.

Mora stares at him. She is somber, her countenance seems very anti–My Little Pony, has venom in her eyes. She says that she only kissed him because she was sure that he had a tiny dick and she didn't want it to hurt her first time. She had talked about it with her psychologist, who'd said it was okay to do that if it helped ease her mind. There isn't anything else to talk about, and he can go; they've broken up, and Sandro the doorman will let him out downstairs. (Later on, thanks to women's magazines like *Ser Única*, Mora would identify her current body language—arms and legs crossed—as unattractive and best avoided.)

Though it was still summer, it was horribly cold in Buenos Aires, a city that seemed taken by surprise every single winter, a winter denial that made their equinoxes all the more humid and painful. In Cassio's mind, the silence was atypical and terrifying. He stopped at a corner. A brightly lit convenience store, and three girls in miniskirts entering, two more coming out. Getting in, getting out, in, out, the old in-out. There must not be anything special about this topological eventuality of penetrating spaces, or things. Or people. Nothing special about it. Nothing at all.

Cassio broke off all relationships with women, starting with the ones in his house. His natural satellites, Sonia and Yolanda, mother and maid, whom he now perceived as inauthentic, united to form an incomprehensibly sadistic caste. The arc of his life coincided with the rise of women, considered a "minority," toward equal civil rights, but his mental life moved in the opposite direction. Soon his room began to stink of pizza and Coca-Cola, sources of essential nutrients for growing young programmers. On the TV, ads showed blue liquids poured onto vaginal products "with wings," which didn't help in the slightest. Was this what they had inside?

Being ugly wasn't his biggest problem; he lacked the least trace of raw animality. The meat that covered Cassio's bones made his body a friendly ensemble: an easygoing mammal without menace. And his mind reacted poorly to the presence of emotions. Already bearing signs of the timidity that would characterize most of his life, Cassio's latest embryonic form was missing the features of manliness indicated by the genes of his Brazilian father, and the fact that Cassio was still short, soft, and Jewish—a mother's goiter of sorts—would send his self-esteem to the bottom of the Mariana Trench of emotions. He asked himself how it was possible that Sonia's womb hadn't rejected him as an enemy alien life-form. Perhaps because this hadn't happened, Cassio had adopted the logic of survivors, renounced masculinity, and mimicked his mother instead. A theory of metabolic racism that assumed the dominance of European genes consumed the darkest hours of his mind.

Moreover, Cassio couldn't understand the interest that Gustavo Levas aroused in his mother. Whenever he detected the man watching television in the living room, he walked rapidly past, and only saw him face-to-face at meals. Gustavo reached out to him several times by talking about computers, but the boy didn't seem impressed. One afternoon when Cassio's mother had gone out, Gustavo approached Cassio with a strange look on his face, and said that the research trip on which he'd met Cassio's mother had been the darkest experience of his life. He wanted to say more, but Cassio's eyes had gone dead, his face expressionless. Gustavo was a public employee, working on the Project at the Ministry of Genetics. "You should come learn about it someday."

Cassio fell into bed wearing only his boxers. He stretched his arm out toward his dresser, neatly ordered in the light of its Yoda lamp. With a black marker he traced a line on his left arm, starting at his armpit and following the principal vein down to where his phalanges joined together. Then he drew the rest of his veins, until the lines were all tangled up in a helicoidal grapevine swirl. He lowered his sky-blue boxers and drew a pair of eyes on his member, which began to rise up in the glow of the cycling, multicolored lights. His old Spectrum clone, disassembled into stacks of cables and circuit boards beside his bed, would be the ship that finally took him back to his true abode: tingling, he prepared himself to enter the mother ship. His ability to disassociate convention from thought would lead to the elite skills noted on his future résumé. He would later create a series of the most violent computer viruses in the history of the country: the Argentine Malvinas.

The feeling of morning sickness always stopped the moment the light entered the window and flowed in slow, carcinogenic rays across Cassio's body. Sometimes Leni stayed over, sprawled out on the bed reading comics and materials from *Página 12*'s School for Young Journalists while Cassio programmed. Relaxed after a game of *Wolfenstein*, Cassio and Leni would sharpen their earliest attempts at misogynist arguments, precarious trenches in the sandbox of resentment. They would later learn that Mora had started "dating" Caca Heller, who now called himself Demián.

Meanwhile, the Buenos Aires ecosystem had become infested with Sinéad O'Connor's "Nothing Compares 2 U" and Whitney Houston's "I Will Always Love You." The mucilaginous furor of "Vision of Love" (Mariah Carey, 1990) still hadn't died down. The only true sweet goodness in the outside world was pooled in a children's television program, *El Show de Xuxa.*

In a series of solitary ceremonies, Cassio connects to the web and wreaks havoc. There is an unforeseen wasp invasion, and he devotes himself to drowning them in a mixture of honey and cream cheese; he watches them sink below the surface still fighting for air, closes his eyes when they stop moving. The servers at his disposal are Ciba and Startel; no machine or human or Ninja Turtle on Earth could face down his implacable attacks on all other life-forms. He listens to the Cure's *Pornography*, and to the songs of Xuxa played backward, especially "Lua de Cristal" (1990), deemed by many the carrier of satanic messages. And he wears a ninja headband.

> *Alert now, make the call, I'm happy now*
> *Beautiful angel of light, I'm happy*
> *He's the leader of invasion, he's the devil of love!*

As Anjodaluz83, Angzt and other nicknames, Cassio Liberman Brandão da Silva would go on to unleash a series of strikes against universities, airline companies, and governmental organizations. They will all give up their most intimate gifts and secrets. A refined repugnance at the ring of asteroids framing his celestial rotations began to gestate within him, but nothing could come between him and his first passion: finding the trapdoors in the code, entering the computers of others.

The better he knew them, the more thoroughly he betrayed them, and the passion birthed a motto: to know is to betray.

He'd begun his climb toward technical mastery by dedicating himself to infiltrating the computers of NASA, searching for proof of extraterrestrial life in the project begun by his supreme idol, Carl Sagan. In the sky, Venus shines through the fog, and the moon dissolves above the crepuscular trench of Buenos Aires.

An expert at leaving her mark on pop music, in the early years of the twenty-first century Madonna began erasing all traces of her time among humans with the technical zeal of a serial killer. If she spent more than five minutes in any given place, a team of people with specialized outfits and equipment arrived to sterilize the area when she left. Her DNA would never again thicken the file folders documenting all those who had bestowed minuscule pieces of skin caught in the concentration of dust, hormones, and sweat that we call life, devoured by the stromatolites of data. Madonna's behavior was pioneering, at a time in which protecting one's overflowing DNA from the drilling of metadata was unthinkable.

Madonna's relationship to the invisible motors of evolution, the *viri*, was the complementary opposite of that of Michael Jackson. Madonna was concerned about the data secreted by the body; Michael, about the data lurking in the world that the body couldn't process. Michael wore a face mask to protect himself, calling attention to the epigenetic environment: his masked appearances pointed out the mysterious trajectories of germs and bacteria, minimal lifeforms menacing the human life. *How much of what one thinks, or does, is in fact the result of the sentinel action of bacteria reacting to their surroundings?* he seemed to be begging to ask. A change was underway, a shift that would have repercussions throughout the planet, with brutal effects comparable to the most violent biological transformations.

At some point between 120 and 190 million years ago, a few cockroaches started to form colonies, began to specialize in the rites of art and war, formed groups devoted to specific tasks such as defending the colony, finding food, and reproducing. Little by little, each group began to generate physical correlates to their given task. Eventually a few colonies learned to domesticate certain types of mushrooms, and started cultivating extensive fungal gardens with which to feed themselves; in this way, new arthropodal forms evolved, and eventually the first super-organism appeared, a bulwark preserving all of the species' varied phases. Later, both humans and insects would create civilizations based formally on the principles of caste—queens, soldiers. And thanks to the LatAm Genetic Data Unification Project, the human population of said zone was able to conceive a new form of existence: united through the traces they'd left, they saw their pasts glow beneath a common light.

The emerging processes that determine the course of history are the product of interactions among immense numbers of individuals, and are themselves shaped by earlier historical variables that are difficult to quantify. Like species united against oblivion, the leading teams of the Genetic Data Unification Project and the Ministry of Genetics worked together on the two known forms of immortality: first, the war of keeping memory alive, transmitted genetically; second, the legacy transmitted through culture. During the Anthropocene, the two forms had become intertwined. Nourished by the gene banks established during the presidency of Raul Alfonsín in Argentina, implemented to help search for those who disappeared during the 1976-1983 dictatorship, the Project helped develop a singularly splendid genetic library.

Like an animal, the human hides in the forest, but it isn't long before it's found.

Having lost trust in the feminine branch of his species, for the next few years Cassio forgot about females altogether. During his final year at ORT Institute of Technology, he audited a Cellular Automatons course, where he studied ways to create tiny armies, multiple hordes whose attacks he planned one day to direct. The class was held in the exact sciences department, on the far side of an ant nest of hallways that Cassio wandered in fascination. He never spoke to anyone, but noted the vague presence of beings more or less similar to himself in the immediate vicinity. And he didn't feel alone.

He was majoring in mathematics, but his latest passions were topology and Ping-Pong. Together they accounted for his scattered moments of leisure, the few hours of free time remaining after his eight-hour exams and his electronic submersions into what he referred to as "personal research." When it wasn't hard at work, his brain became lethargic, like a snake after a large meal; in the jungle, snakes live in profound anonymity, only allow themselves to be seen as they attack, then languish in supine vulnerability, and this is when their mortality rate spikes. Cassio thought about the errors that subjugate the world, and their terrifying naturalization; about the calm acceptance of evil, as if it were merely a substitute for the law of gravity. He let his hair grow down to his shoulders, began dressing all in black. When it rained he sheathed himself in a duckling-yellow raincoat; walking through the parks on campus, he looked like a huge plastic bumblebee.

Among other highlights of his nerdy life, he had an affair with numbers theory, which addressed many of the problems at the base of cryptography—his airy love—and was friendly with two Asian students, Shiro and Coco, whose Ping-Pong supremacy was overwhelming. Pavilion 1 of Exact Sciences bustled with activity, but it was rare to see the same faces around for long: the most gifted brains soon abandoned the university, as did the most desperate, which is how they caught up with the most gifted. The capital needed beings like him and his Ping-Pong colleagues, and was in a position to make them better offers.

As photophobic as any albino crab, Cassio avoided the outside world whenever he could. His lair was a third-floor laboratory on the shaded side of Exact Sciences. The world unfolded in all directions, coursed through the channels surrounding him, but never established direct contact. He hadn't yet graduated when he was offered a position as a cryptography assistant in the computer science department—his debut as a subordinate. His boss, Héctor Skilnov, was a "Scientific Computer," and had the diploma to prove it; the field had stopped producing his type in the mid-1980s. Scientific knowledge relies on hierarchical structures with clear chains of command; each order given is a display of attenuated brute strength. Cassio's job, which he found both easy and enjoyable, consisted of preparing Skilnov's classes, and giving the lectures when Skilnov didn't show up, which was most of the time.

It was during this period that he wrote his first seminal work in natural language, "F.A.T.S.O." (Finite Algebraic

Transform Scrambler in O[log n]). It earned him waves of popularity among the most renowned nerds. His Dead Kennedys T-shirts disappeared, replaced by T-shirts bearing mathematical symbols.

Now Cassio strode ominously into the student center, HACKER OR SERF flaring across his chest. In the café, he ordered a sandwich with no lettuce. The boy at the register bowed his head in respect.

"Ave Cassius."

It was Maiki. He'd founded a university political organization united against political organizations; it was called NO, a sort of absolutist Trotskyite super league. Cassio first met him in Mathematical Analysis; he decided he liked Maiki. Maiki was probably even more isolated from society than Cassio was, distancing himself from his natural allies at the speed of light.

Maiki was blond and extremely pale. He spoke without moving his eyebrows, and rarely blinked; at times his hands emitted dissonant signals, parallel messages that were independent of the transmission coming from north of his neck. He spent his summers in Israel shepherding goats and collecting oranges in the occupied deserts of the Negev; he returned wearing brown jackets with the word DEFENSE written in Hebrew. Loyal to anarcho-nerd folklore, he allowed the conceptual violence of his T-shirts to impose itself on his surroundings.

For Maiki, revolutions were possible, but required a specific diagnostic of the system's bugs. Cassio agreed that the university (known to others as the universe) was running on diseased software. Maiki had managed a few small subversive attacks. He'd had salami pizza delivered to the homes of professors, from different pizza joints, delivery pizza version of a DDoS attack; during a conference in the Aula Magna, he'd sent small homemade drones fitted with dildos traversing through the air. Ridding the world of senior management wasn't enough, he said—but it was necessary.

Maiki ended up shaken by exchanges like this, his eyes shining in a way that was not quite normal; the passage of language through his body left him exhausted. Cassio returned to the problems of his thesis, and Maiki withdrew toward his inner hominid, in search of solace.

Cassio was working on the design of a constellation of autonomous agents: sleeper cells, latent, perfectly invisible, scattered throughout public third-party servers all over the world. It would be impossible for anyone to know what the cells were waiting for; that is, no one could possibly guess which of the universe's signals would provoke something similar to a *behavior*. Cassio's thesis project had a number of innovative features, and made him an extremely favorable prospect for a doctorate in cryptography. It described a set of algebraic transformations whose properties permitted the conception of a new type of algorithm based on public key encryption, a form of computation that could be used to hide complex processes on public servers under the very noses of their users. When the moment came and the proper set of signals was sent, the encrypted algorithms on the dark side of the globe would begin to execute their code, setting off on the mission they'd been built to carry out.

The method shared similarities with several emerging

biological mechanisms wherein the sudden appearance of a key—an enzyme, an extremely specific temperature, the presence of a natural enemy—sets fundamental processes in motion; in some cases, the process involves the leap to a new formulation of existence. This was the idea with which Cassio had begun his personal research, back when he was playing with the notion of experimenting with the new generation of robust, powerful algorithms designed to penetrate security systems at critical moments without human intervention—algorithms that could learn from their own mistakes, abandoning paths as necessary in order to try others. His billions of data drones could carry on with their algorithmic lives without ever revealing the secret programming they held within; strictly speaking, they could *dedicate themselves to normality* as they awaited the call to begin the superordinate procedures for which they had been created.

It was an extremely beautiful idea. The algorithms were like golems, their bodies hidden in the high grass of data, awaiting the key that would turn them into something monstrous, potentially beyond control. Cassio spent hour after hour looking for any errors he might have made—future vulnerabilities against which to innoculate his creatures. Then he went to see Skilnov, his immediate superior.

Cassio—the cotton T-shirt that covered his sweaty torso still shouting, HACKER OR SERF—corralled Skilnov in the elevator. He gave Skilnov a general sketch of the idea, then poked around a bit, inspecting the man's facial barricade. Cassio knew that his army was perfect, that his technique was flawless and brilliant. The intensity with which he breathed into Skilnov's face could well indicate that he sought human confirmation of his status as a prodigious crypto-eminence, but in fact, more than anything, he was just looking for someone to talk to. He thought of a Borges poem, of the part where the rabbi gazes fearfully, humanly, at the golem:

> *The Rabbi looked at it with tenderness*
> *and a bit of horror. How, he asks, could I*
> *have begotten this pathetic child,*
> *abandoning my source of sanity—my idleness?*

Skilnov's vague reply takes him by surprise; the man doesn't seem to fully understand. He makes a few incoherent suggestions, which Cassio, a bit impatient, dismisses without pretending otherwise. But the graft doesn't take long to germinate, albeit in other directions. A few days later, Lara Müller, an assistant professor, asks him to meet her for coffee at Selquet.

The bar's mirrors surround undulant lacquered furniture. The decor hasn't changed since 1975—a warm penumbra, transmitter of intimacy. Cassio was the only one there wearing a T-shirt; he appeared to float through the seductive low light like a fat kid with a case of ostranenie. Lara was wearing a tight, navy blue sweater that showed off her form. The waiter came quickly to take their order.

"A beer," she said. "You too? My treat."

Lara looked into his eyes and smiled. Her hair fell to her collarbones, which disappeared at the edge of the blue wool. Blonde, gray eyes, she'd be eight years or so older than him;

a friendly and intelligent face, which only the gray academic surroundings could ever have blurred. Lara belonged to the aristocracy of Argentine science: her parents (young male professor, gifted female student) had met in a physics university classroom, both with patents of their own, and she had proceeded brilliantly up the tunnel that connects the Nacional Buenos Aires to the mathematics department. Cassio, unfortunately, lacked the instincts and self-esteem necessary to perceive the very real possibility of carnal insertion there before him.

Their mugs of beer arrived, with a plate of salty snacks and olives; Cassio entertained himself building little peanut pathways. A number of unaccompanied men looked over at them from time to time, but Lara didn't seem to notice, focused as she was on the conversation. She told Cassio about a new fellowship that had just opened up; with his grades and a recommendation from Skilnov, this coming year he'd be eligible for a research post at CONICET. He could work in numbers theory; she could take him on as a research assistant, she added with imploring eyes. It would be a first step toward setting the shape of his life for the coming decades. He would have time to do personal research as well, as the overall workload would never overwhelm an intellect like his; and, who knows, he could soon become the head of a research team; without a doubt, getting Skilnov's recommendation in the bank would be worth the trouble.

It was Cassio's turn. He talked for a bit about his thesis, explained the implications of his bot army and the advantages for humanity of full encryption; his troops would spread out around the world, silent, infiltrating everything, would form a vast field of distributed execution for code yet to come— infinitely malleable, an encyclopedia of virus species, each with its specific mutational capabilities. Cassio envisioned his tiny dark armies permeating every interconnected object within the numeric universe, every machine that humans use to interface; his creatures would exceed anything people thought of as real, or even as possible. Born in computerized environments, they would be capable of penetrating biological ones; nothing could stop them from taking on new forms and heading in new directions. Given the profile of his forces, he could establish whole new fields of analysis, could program systems that would extend his troops' capacity for shadowy destruction far into the coming decades.

Cassio had talked a great deal without really taking stock of what he was saying, and something about Lara's rigid lips projected a sense of fear. They were quiet for a few moments. Eventually Lara offered that his thesis project sounded extremely promising. Cassio finished eating his peanut pathways, and looked directly into her gray eyes. They radiated a blurred density, like a fluorescent coral reef on the ocean floor.

They walked out of the Selquet and headed up La Pampa, past the privet hedge of a love hotel. As far as Lara was concerned, sex with Cassio would be a completely benign experience; even if they ended up working together, it would never become uncomfortable, as she belonged to the set of people who had no trouble disassociating from their bodies, and would find life unimaginable on any other terms. Her hand now brushed against Cassio's, and he felt the full discharge of the electric prod of passion. He closed his eyes, became a fistful of retinas; the idea that a woman would *offer* herself to him was on the order of science fiction. Once the shock had passed, Cassio steadied his stride and returned to the topic of his thesis. But he didn't dare look at her, and Lara was hardly going to drag him anywhere.

Cassio now brought maniacal focus to his writing. He was stalked by an enormous wave of tedium, a tsunami of disdain for everything around him; the coarse voice of darkness had returned to descend upon him. He had to fend off the tenebrous particles that swept across the swamp of his mind in flurries of black emptiness, much like the terrifying advent of Nothing in his favorite film, *The NeverEnding Story* (W. Petersen, 1984). In the film, Atreyu has to save his world from destruction by defeating the most formidable villain imaginable. And like Atreyu, Cassio was working against the clock.

But even under the virulent reign of Nothing, the world of Cassio was still, like the subject of his thesis, a springtime of possibilities. As Cassio explained to Harpo, his turtle: "I want to partition my brain, let part of it compile other things, work on my personal research. But I clearly have to participate in life in some way." One option was to take a position as chief hacking officer at some obscure digital organization, make thirty thousand dollars a month, and move to Dubai as a young professional within the New World Order. (He was still far from imagining the uses to which his talents could be put as part of the LatAm project.)

Mundane pleasures populated the path of computerized evil. Jeipi, one of his old comrades in arms at Satanic Brain, was nowhere to be found in any legal or fiscal database. He hijacked the botnets of others and administered his own: he had hundreds of thousands of zombie computers under his control, and activated them a few hundred at a time or all at once according to the dictates of his masters. He carried out the mass infections—gonorrhea was one of his most contagious hits—from the comfort of his own home; by night he worked on his next virus at the latest fashionable dive bar, and turned into moth bait.

Others, like Phil, had chosen to become a different sort of ghost. Originally from Montpellier, Phil lived outside a village deep in the French countryside, in a house with no internet connection. He looked after his goats, which he'd named after the players on France's 1998 World Cup championship team, and sold their cheese online—down in the village there was a boulangerie with Wi-Fi. He made different varieties of Pélardon using truffles that he grew himself, and each variety came in a package decorated with a pixelated portrait of one of the goats; Zidane and Trezeguet were among the most popular. The technique required for each new attack developed silently in his mind over time; when the idea matured, became inexorable, he rode his bike into town, and in an hour or two had wreaked havoc. He then bought a few freshly baked rolls, and rode back to his house and his cheeses. He was impossible to trace, and often donated credit for his attacks to Anonymous—a modus operandi that would lend identity and vigor to that group in the years to come.

And what sort of ghost should Cassio himself become? Spirit captain of encrypted insects, or phantom demiurge of maniac bots? Financially speaking, any version of the ghostly hacker life had its complications: a far more pressing issue than those raised in ethical disquisitions was the fact that it's hard to get paid on the path of evil. It was essential to establish trustworthy relationships with the golden circles of the digital underworld, which implied close proximity to the practical aspect of illegality, which had never interested Cassio precisely because of his purist pretensions. Hacking was a brilliant endeavor because the act of developing perfect bombs for spaces occupied by mistakes was itself brilliant. Mocking corporate armies, spitting on the sense of security felt by those who believed themselves to hold power—subjecting them, in sum, to a new reality principle wherein beings like Cassio reigned—all this was crucial by definition, was the purest societal endeavor his brain had ever undertaken. Lowering himself to industrial espionage, to contacting "interested parties" in pursuit of financial gain, would inevitably be tinged with vulgarity. Much as in the classical definitions of art, the notion of utility defiled one's actions, tearing off the halo of purity that signified their depth and beauty. It was therefore not a matter of moral principle that kept Cassio off the path of evil, but rather a certain aesthetic intuition similar to the one that had led him to reject applied forms of mathematics, such as physics: it seemed intolerable to him that things could only be thought to exist within the world of objects, and according to its rules; that they could only be considered true if they resided within that particular sphere of human possibility; that their theoretical perfection alone wasn't enough to make them real.

The idea of a world of rational actors motivated by romantic/ cerebral ideals and fulfilling their potential by exploiting weaknesses was what inspired the euphoric baroque phase of utopian liberalism in the 1990s; Cassio formed part of this world in intimate if marginal ways. The central imperative was to find the error, the crack through which to enter; doing so ensured him access to zones which only a very specific elite were skilled enough to transit. The alleged normality of the world had never been on his side, so why start honoring it now?

In spite of his aesthetic misgivings regarding both the path of evil and the illicit activities carried out in certain parts of the exclusive zones to which he had entry, Cassio did make occasional exceptions. For a time he entertained himself by building digital security systems for Comando Vermelho, the czars of the underworld in Rio de Janeiro. With their extremely white tennis shoes, their Ithaca shotguns, and their child-stoner faces, he thought of them as angels from Mars. He invented a way to communicate with them through the game of Doom: when they found him in the labyrinth, he gave them an email address that would self-destruct in twenty-four hours; outside the game, there was no way for them to reach him. And when they were jailed for trafficking as part of the government's drive to clean up the city, it was easy for Cassio to disappear like smoke.

For several weeks thereafter he followed the news closely. He accompanied the twilight of his former Carioca colleagues by creating depressive user profiles and using them to leave violent commentaries on videos that celebrated these men as armed saviors; the men seemed even more infantile to him now than they had before, which in turn made the universe of law feel ever stupider and more worthy of disdain. Nature is horrifying precisely because it bears witness to the vileness of humankind; it waits, arms crossed, for our extinction. And if the men's brains managed to survive their jail sentences, at least they'd find their money waiting for them on the far side of the labyrinth Cassio had so lovingly built, its exit path leading to a safety deposit box in a bank in the British Virgin Islands.

He started swimming every day. He'd arrive at the gym in Belgrano with his sky-blue Adidas bag, put on a checkered bathing suit one size too small, and walk like a giant in flip-flops past the immense window of the gym where women in tight sports outfits and ponytails drank Gatorade. Cassio positioned his toes perpendicular to the edge of the pool and imagined a tall building, the wind, death's power to absorb. He let himself fall headfirst, his arms rigid at his sides, and the red numbers of the clock on the wall dissolved in the chlorinated water that took him in, protecting him from the shifting clouds of cologne and aftershave above. A few meters away, barracuda schools of children added their liquids to the pool. Little by little he lost his human form. Sometimes, underwater, he saw strange shapes, as if he were swimming in a placenta full of monsters, the way life must have felt in the blue fields where he squirmed and floated before being born.

In general he preferred to swim late in the day, when the only other swimmers were older ladies and groups of pregnant women, cretaceous amphibians gamboling about as he watched from beneath the surface, their bodies iterating over and over for hours. He imagined seaweed twisting around elongated, toeless feet. Sometimes the image persisted beneath his daily thoughts until well into the night, and he woke with an invisible knife in his hand.

When he returned to the world's surface, the sun avoided direct contact with the subcutaneous irruptions on his face, those silent aspartame distillates of his organism, fruit of the modified feces of *E. coli*. Movement on the surface connected to movement in the depths. His orifices opened and his senses enlarged. He could feel the motors of cars several blocks away as they sped up or slowed down, and the rumble of the kiosk freezers, and the whisper of the stacks of air conditioners that climbed the sides of the towers; he saw the entire world as if it were submerged. Shoals swimming across Soldado de la Independencia Street, crossing Santa Fe Avenue and Pacífico. Clouds of krill drifting down Maure Street; eels tangled up at the moss-green lights; the sky covered with sheets of plankton. It was a world of slow, insensate beings.

Each night advanced its refutation of the light, and Cassio put off going home. He would walk up and down along Báez and Chenaut, occasionally finding himself on the far side of Libertador near Bolivia Square. The shadows of those smoking dope with their hoods on, and the glint of eyes looking up at him from ground level: these were transmissions in Morse code, to which the nerdity of his fluorescent skin responded intermittently in the dark. One night he found some broken dolls, glimpsed movement and nudity behind the bushes, but wasn't able to see any organs that interested him.

It was with a certain yearning that he caressed the possibility of dedicating himself to speculative computing—of devoting himself wholly to the creation of digital armadas that were ever more singular and complex. He and his creatures could all take shelter beneath the university's mantle of invisibility, could circulate with impunity in the mode of *possibility*. But the idea of having to talk to Skilnov again, of most likely having to depend on the man's acquiescence, was just too depressing. Maybe Maiki was right: maybe the whole world had to be hacked—and of all possible worlds, he would have to find one worth the trouble of hacking.

Cassio didn't want to be alone with just his computer and his turtle; part of him was desperate for the touch of other beings. He knew that Shiro and Coco had left the university to work at a gamer company, and that the company was looking for more programmers. He sent an email. Without even interviewing him, they offered him a job. And he accepted.

The albino crabs begin to migrate, pursuing the sun. The massive grayish gathering could be seen from an altitude of thirty kilometers—the darkness from which the crabs came had changed; they could no longer breathe inside it. Movements on the surface connect to movements in the depths. Those on the surface are accompanied by invisible contrary forces, each with its own vectors and subterranean aims. Given the finite nature of the human era, eventually they come to dominate the culture as brutally as the ravages of nature.

In the 1960s, a group of young people tries to randomize their actions: they aim to separate their existence from the masses, the mainstream. They are known as hippies, their collective attempt is to ignore the laws established by their parents. But how to break a law inherited en masse? Their rebellion consists of inserting moments of chaos into established patterns of conduct; they call these randomizations "liberty." A plan to become unique by generating an unrepeatable life pattern modulates their behavior; the noisy surface of the 1960s and '70s moves erratically through the cities and insists on its "revolutionary" status.

At a deeper, more silent level, another group of brilliant and impatient young people is giving birth to a more silent eclosion: a turn toward abstraction. They lay no claim to revolutionary status: they are in fact conservative, even square. Though they do have a precise sense of lifestyle, their chosen battlefield has nothing to do with musical tastes, political

tendencies, sexual habits, or fashion. It will be the conserva-
tives that will lead an insurrection ascendent and long lasting
in the fundamental makeup of capital.

In the following decade, the obscure conservative heroes
of this generation will begin by disassociating money from its
backing in gold. Little by little, paper currency will draw for
itself a curve that grows ever more distant from its reference—
a tendency shared by abstract and conceptual art. At the center
of these tendencies, a new legal and theoretical structure will
slowly come into being, one that will lead to the financial
revolution of the 1980s, and in the years that follow, will allow
for contortions and iterations at greater and greater levels of
abstraction, building one on the next, consuming themselves
as they go, until capital is virtualized into what it was always
meant to be: a self-generating ouroboros of bits.

The movement's early resonant hits will sing of the rise of
Wall Street—of the decline of traditional economic resource-
fulness in favor of corporate restructuring and junk bonds.
But Wall Street will be just a rite of passage: the separation of
money from its backing in gold will reach new highs and lows
with the securitization of debt and derivatives and the collapse
of September 2008. Only a few days after the fall of Lehman
Brothers, in October of that year, the phoenix of capital would
begin to rise again with the publication of "Bitcoin: a peer-
to-peer electronic cash system," and the legend of Satoshi
Nakamoto will birth the blockchain. Completely void of any
connection to anything real, money will find its true Hegelian
self in cryptocurrency. A consciousness of its own.

One movement works as the surface, where visible change

occurs; the other movement is the structure, hidden beneath the flow of mortal life. The two movements—hippie/randomizing and financial/conservative—share a disdain for industrial corporations and factories, the former because industry embodies the values of their parents, which they are obliged to reject, and the latter because industry entails a theory of value that competes with the absolute liberalism that the poetic flight of capital (Viz. ever more distant from the gold standard) seeks for itself. And both movements endeavor to rise beyond the guiding industrial paradigm of progress. Their hearts bear the mark of technology.

"I've never met a DAN in person! Digital Anarchy!"

On Santi Pando's T-shirt, a young Bill Gates is smoking a joint beside a vintage computer.

"You were there when it started, right?"

Cassio's smile stretches his lips but doesn't show his teeth. Pando, CEO of Ship.e.bo, can't hide his excitement:

"I didn't really know them—well, I *knew* that they were super elite, but I was too young—I was probably still playing with my Playmobil while everything was going on! I might as well have been one of those little Playmobil figures, but Jako, do you know Jako? He went out with Wari's sister, who'd been in school with Mat from DAN more or less around the time when they fucked up the main server at the IRS. Do you know Jako?"

At a nearby desk, a girl with pink hair follows the scene with interest. Bunkered down behind an enormous Mac monitor, she's talking on the telephone and staring at the latest arrival. Cassio nods at the image of Bill respectfully, and manages one word:

"No."

"Well, sure, I didn't think you'd know him—shit, it's obvious you wouldn't—but he knew about you. What an awesome time. Dude, it's awesome that you've come to work with us. Really. You're exactly what we want—it's, like, very *aspirational* for us to have you here. In the good sense of the word, obviously. I don't want to sound like an ass-kisser, but it's true! You know, in our line of work a criminal record's worth more than a résumé."

Santi Pando made a *T* with his hands, and flew toward the back storeroom.

It was a cute little office in "Palermo Valley," the nucleus for tech start-ups in Buenos Aires: an old house, recently recycled, where the atmosphere was relaxed and the exposed brick contrasted with the black monitors. No one there was over the age of twenty-five. Only the one girl in sight had a Mac. There was a vintage sky-blue refrigerator, and orange chairs around a tall table holding fruit and granola bars. On one wall, the enormous mouth of a girl (not the same one) stuck out her tongue above the Ship.e.bo logo—a haphazard collage on an ad for ice cream.

Someone touches his back; it's the girl with pink hair.

"Neese to might you," she says, without taking the sucker out of her mouth.

The sucker forms a little ball at the base of her cheek—a GIF that would inspire subsequent skirmishes between Cassio and his gonads. Now Pando comes running back toward them, his hands full of Cokes:

"Ha. Ninja Turtles!"

Hidden behind his purple mask, Donatello waves from Cassio's cotton-covered belly. Santi winks and holds up the Cokes.

"The team is excellent, you'll see. We're exactly what we look like—all we do is program. Even when we're not here, we're still programming, but in our minds! There's free Cokes and chocolate and granola bars for all the programmers. I'm going to order Ninja Turtle candy! Coke Zero or regular?"

After a few experiments with David Beckham–style

minicrests, among other attempts to reprocess his in-person viscosity into something a little more memorable, CEO Santi Pando had recently gone back to the bowl cut of his childhood, which complemented his thick eyeglasses and ironic corporate T-shirts. Santi was perfectly aware that he lacked a mystic element: he came from a wealthy family, a childhood of neckties in English-speaking private schools, and he'd missed out on the poetic adolescence of authentic hackers who spent their era of sebaceous explosions writing BBS posts and defying the law. In the 1990s, he and his friends had seen their houses inundated by technology; the country had just thrown open the door to foreign imports, bringing in not just computers but also the yogurt makers and other appliances that were all the rage in Argentina back then.

Santi tried to compensate for his lack of magic with an entrepreneurial style based on hyperkinesis, ayahuasca trips, enthusiasm, and anxiety. He defined himself as a *devigner*—half developer and half designer—a pampered, middle-class business child. He gave the very best of himself in interviews:

"What was the name of your first girlfriend?"

"Commodore 64."

"What's your dream?"

"To create a collective innovation platform that allows the web to attain consciousness."

"What's the sexiest thing about the internet? (Without mentioning porn!)"

"My favorite porn is people building Web applications—a living, breathing, creative community of geeks!"

* * *

In the photograph that accompanied the profile, Santi was dressed as a Stormtrooper. He hadn't been able to convince Alan Rochenforr, his angel investor, to pose next to him as Han Solo. "Now that I'm an investor, I'm on the dark side, so I can only be Darth Vader," had been Rochenforr's excuse.

"Come here. I want you to meet Alan."

Cassio and Santi drained their Cokes, each taking the measure of the other in a moment of intense silence. Like in a Western, Santi cracked his neck joints and Cassio shifted his weight from one leg to the other. Then they climbed up the staircase at the edge of a patio whose center held a lime tree.

Alan Rochenforr was walking on a treadmill. He had his earpiece in, was on a call. He made a T with his hands.

Rochenforr belonged to the world of pure capital, which only occasionally intersected with the productive/creative world of which Santi Pando considered himself the captain. Though Rochenforr didn't visit the Ship.e.bo office very often, he liked to keep his own desk there, with photos—blond children with braces, and a pregnant woman submerged up past her genitals in some lake in Uruguay. It made him feel close to youth and passion. Now forty-five years old, Alan Rochenforr had met every expectation for beings of his class: he had graduated from Harvard, founded a Latino copycat of an American company, managed to sell it before the dot-com crash, and could now dedicate himself to paying for his architect wife's art courses and supervising the growth of his free-range offspring. He continued to bet on the future, and hoped that this start-up would catch hold of *something* as yet unnamed but already present in the world. When he invested in a company, he always asked that there be a room with a treadmill—he had one in Barracas, and one in Puerto Madero. This was how he ensured that his visits would be worthwhile at the intracellular level.

Now he dried his head and patted his hands on his shirt.

"How's it going, man? Santi told me a lot about you."

Alan glanced at the Ninja Turtles on Cassio's T-shirt, and Cassio showed his teeth. Sometimes he liked to show his teeth, or pretend to be a robot, or hold someone's gaze.

"It's a pleasure to meet such an eminence. Welcome to the team."

Alan dried his hand and held it out. He mentioned that on average he ran three kilometers a day during his calls. He wiped the towel across his face and paused the treadmill, then drew his face tight into something resembling a smile.

It was decidedly nontrivial that Ship.e.bo was the first video game to star a native Indo-American community. The game was highly original, an attractive option for demanding users who liked to entertain themselves during the workday by throwing endangered natives around. It was inspired by dwarf-throwing games (always set pointedly in the US, Canada, medieval France, or England), and was designed to gather a critical mass of users the company could then channel toward new offerings. This would in turn render vast amounts of user data that could later be resold to avid marketing directors at other companies.

Each native successfully thrown was converted into a donation to be sent to IRL Ship.e.bo communities—this was the touch of marketing genius that had led Rochenforr to invest in the company. Santi liked to say that it wasn't a business, it was a movement. And now Rochenforr begged their pardon, said he had to make another call.

When they came back downstairs, Cassio looked hopefully at the reception desk. The girl with grapefruit-colored hair smiled and typed in his direction.

That afternoon, Cassio was introduced to the movement's arcana. For example, Santi taught him the secret handshake: one hand approached another, and together they formed an undulant, snakelike *S*. It ended with a snap of the fingers.

The vernacular Web held other novelties for Cassio, ones that would be received enthusiastically by his timid glands. Outside of a few flings, the active life of his meaty joystick could hardly be called gregarious, propelled as it was by sessions of self-love that Cassio never allowed himself to think of as pleasure. His emotional capacities were those of an unweaned infant; the long delay of his access to female organs had contributed exponentially to his idealization thereof. The lives of overly romantic individuals are often corroded by the possibility of love; though this was not his case, he too had set the entry barrier for anyone interested in taking possession of him—in becoming the master of his will—exceptionally low.

In another time and place, a nerd like Cassio would have suffered. He would have spent his entire gray existence off to one side of the office, taking orders from inferior beings, shoved into the worm section of the ego food chain. But rumors about the presence of a hacking eminence spread like napalm: his past provided him with a top-drawer superhero cape. His disheveled look was a necessary counterpoint to his hidden magic, an inverted image of his interior worth. Much as the dream of capital had projected muscle-bound genies surging from detergent bottles and household appliances for the women of the previous century, the challenges women faced in the early years of the twenty-first century created new needs and thus new holes—new vulnerabilities into which manhood could be inserted. Girls were always having trouble with their computers. Cassio would be the domestic genius, the whiz kid who was always willing to help. He now felt the rebirth of a masculine vigor that had, strictly speaking, never been born in the first place—a starry ascent within his own sexual niche.

Melina had studied musical comedy. She changed her hair color every week, dressed in eye-catching outfits that she designed herself, and took care of her administrative tasks with relaxed efficiency. From Monday to Friday she was the only woman in the Ship.e.bo office; on the weekends she took part in sporadic performances of indie plays on off-off-Corrientes. When she first met Cassio, the work in question was *Vampires on Facebook: The Musical.*

At an office party thrown to celebrate Ship.e.bo's five thousandth user, Cassio stood at the bar as if clinging to the edge of the deep end of a swimming pool. The rest of the programmers socialized around him. And the universe found itself in an advanced state of affairs: there were several girls at the party that he'd never seen before.

"Your name is Casio, like the watch?"

"But with two *Ses.*"

"And you give the time?"

"I'll give it to you if you want."

When Melina mischievously extends the secret handshake in his direction, Cassio moves in counter to the vertigo he feels, and kisses her on the cheek. In his mind he works through the key teachings of his friend Jeipi, who has the most experience with women of anyone he knows: even in a cabaret, surrounded by prostitutes, it's crucial *not to show the slightest interest.* A woman's self-esteem can only be stimulated through her vanity—Jeipi had underlined this in the air. Minimize your actions; make sure all responsibility for the scene ends up on her shoulders. It was the only thing Cassio had ever learned about feminism, and it was enough.

Melina smiles publicly:

"And aside from giving the time, what else do you know how to do?"

"I can create languages. I can derail banks. I can create invisible armies unlike anything modern computers have ever experienced. And I can give you the time."

Still holding a slice of lemon in her mouth, Melina laughs, and whispers something in his ear; Cassio doesn't catch it but doesn't ask, focused as he is on the viscous gurgling around his *corpus cavernosum,* watchtower and lighthouse for the human night. Melina is practically hanging all over Cassio the Stoic. Then a friend of hers shows up, and the two women head off to the bathroom. They come back out smiling, their arms around each other's shoulders; they head out to the street and hail a taxi. They laugh too loudly and their hair is a mess, but none of that matters to them at all. Cassio keeps thinking that he should jot down the car's license plate, but instead he just memorizes it; another girl talks to him, yet another girl kisses him, and the night is shattered by invisible asteroids.

The following Monday, in the office bathroom, Cassio's hands advance like interstellar capsules across Melina's mammary terrain: *Mariner I* and *II*, launched simultaneously to capture samples of the Venusian atmosphere. With her blouse half-open, Melina breathes heavily against the tile. In a fit of passion, Cassio nibbles at her neck through the collar of the jacket she's wearing. She responds by ensnaring him with her legs; her fuchsia panties come into brief contact with his belly button and the tentacular hair below. He does his best to focus on Diego Armando Maradona so as not to finish too soon.

After a couple of weeks of surreptitious encounters in the bathroom and after work—they can't meet on weekends, when Art requires her presence—Cassio invites Leni to join him at the Abasto to see *Vampires on Facebook: The Musical*. Melina appears onstage, and Cassio takes a deep breath; Melina opens her mouth to sing (Radiohead's "We Suck Young Blood," accompanied by a ukulele), and Cassio clutches at the armrests. His heart (because he has one, almost as present and porous as what throbs farther down) stops. She is without a doubt the play's most beautiful vampire, a fact that must not have escaped the cognitive apparatus of the director, because her character takes off all her clothes, twice. This bothers Cassio, who can't stop obsessing over what must go on during rehearsals. Leni declares himself "amazed" because the play is "competitively terrible," a nontrivial fact not because most plays are terrible but because at a certain point it becomes difficult to distinguish one degree of awfulness from another. Cassio looks at him, his eyes full of hate. He grumbles a little, but without much conviction.

Outside the theater exit, willows hang like stage curtains across Humahuaca Street. Leni and Cassio crouch down behind some cars, peering through the branches. The door spits out batches of people in costumes; Cassio's mouth fills with saliva. On that urban tundra, Melina looks like a ghost, her eyes painted red and black. The long green leaves, the streetlights, the flying cockroaches: everything conspires together to make her even more painfully beautiful. What was he hoping to accomplish? He decides to become his own Voyager, bearer of an incomprehensible message launched into outer space.

Then Melina comes walking up the line of cars.

"Hey, what are you guys doing?"

His invisibility cape dissolves.

Their shoulders still hunched, Cassio and Leni come out of their hiding place. They exchange a brief look, but since they've already been exposed as idiots, they can now relax. Melina plants kisses on their cheeks, takes Cassio by the hand; her other hand tenses in her pocket. Leni follows along behind.

"They came to see the play!" she announces to her cohort.

The silence lowers gloomily from the trees. The actors stare at Cassio's midsection, where a Ninja Turtle is making a "*V for Vendetta*" sign.

"Our next play should have Ninja Turtles," says one of them.

Another half stifles a derisive laugh. Melina introduces Cassio as "a friend," and he murmurs something that isn't quite hello. The actors disperse, only to regroup farther away. Cassio decides that the problem isn't just that they are *actors*— a synonym for loathsome, according to Leni—but also that he doesn't like them at all.

Cassio had recently begun cultivating a project involving homemade microdrones with a pair of cronies he'd met in his Cellular Automatons course, Karsa and Vila. The three of them gathered in a borrowed garage on Rosetti Street in Chacarita. Proof of the feasibility of minuscule flying machines was abundant in the form of insects; affixed with cameras and microphones, the drones' potential within the world of espionage was obvious. He'd thought of testing them out on some pretty neighbor, but wasn't sure he had any; in any case, that was a minor problem compared to the technical challenge in question.

As noted, in times past Cassio found projects set in the real world to be irredeemably vulgar. The microdrones were his first attempt at creating physical machines relegated to sharing space with humans: he'd just dropped out of his mathematics program, and had started to feel the physical necessity of building things with his hands, to hear the call of the empiric emanating from deep inside.

Just then the phone in his pocket began to vibrate. Cassio stared at the screen:

hey what time is it?

He answered immediately:

Whatever time you want.

He waited.

Kkkkkk.

Now she was typing something else.

IM HOME ALL ALONE WANNA COME?

Impressed, Karsa and Vila iterated around him in silence. A midnight text, void of meandering, stripped of civic masks, could only signify an interest both specific and sexual. Pearlescent with prestige, Cassio said his goodbyes and flew to her on his moped.

Melina opened the door, dreamlike, wearing only a white undershirt and a thin miniskirt. She kissed him on the cheek and offered him a shot of local vodka; she asked if he had pot, and Cassio shook his head.

"It's so great that you came," she said, smiling, backing away from him.

She tripped and landed on the bed. Maybe she was over-acting her drunkenness a bit, or maybe not; the flow of seductive signals continued uninterrupted. Cassio did his best to mimic her smile and state of relaxation, but the internal pressure of his liquid DNA had compromised his entire being quite painfully—he could barely breathe through the little hole at the end of his erection. The computer played Radiohead's "Subterranean Homesick Alien" and lit their bodies with flashes of lunar light. Melina stretched out on the bed and finished her joint; her vagina, unsheltered beneath her miniskirt, flickered luminous above him.

None of his life's previous mental landscapes had prepared him for the microscopic spectacle of the glistening humidity gathered in those minuscule valleys. He fell to his knees, careful not to look directly at this eyeless fish, this mini–Jabba the Hut in its throne room. He opened his mouth, felt a vortex of suction twist his lips. He imagined the hypothetical ingestion of an extremely soft and airy muffin, sending his tongue in on an exploratory mission to capture a bit of filling. Melina emitted a series of strange sounds, and then her voice faded away.

He asked if she was asleep. She didn't answer.

Cassio's mouth was now numb—she had apparently applied some spermicidal lubricant. Cassio raised his eyes to her incandescent Mac, still sending its rays of light across the bed. A few days before, he'd installed the latest operating system and a few little programs to help her avoid leaving traces on the internet. He hadn't yet checked to see if they were running properly.

Her Facebook page was open. There were several messages from Marto, one of the actors from the musical. The little arrows of her messages curved toward his—she'd answered every one. The odds of a musical comedy actor being heterosexual were extremely low, but to judge from Marto's photos—that bulge—and the content of his messages, it

seemed indisputable that he was. Cassio made a few cal-
culations, ones that even someone without his privileged
mathematical cranial hemisphere could have managed. The
data were clear: what he'd eaten was a muffin full of Marto's
genetic leftovers from, technically, just a few hours ago, a
thought Cassio found thoroughly unpleasant.

He left his moped leaned up against a light post, and entered
the office without making a sound. The human beings had
all dispersed, leaving only the sisterhood of machines, the
blinking LED lights, and the hum of his own breathing. He
was having trouble seeing the outlines, the solid spirits of
things; he sat down at his desk to wait for his energy to dissipate. He rested his hands on the desk's melamine veneer; he
felt nauseous, his own magma trying to decide out of which
hole to erupt. He drank a little water, tried to calm himself
down.

He imagined himself puking up Melina's Mac, the office's
nervous system transmitting the acid to all the terminals—this
scorched the circuit boards, integrating them into a stew of
biological waste—and then a dry flash as each power source
imploded. His elbow brushed against the trackpad of his computer, and the screen lit up. In green Helvetica the words read,
"In 2020 we will either be Hackers or Serfs." His headboard
phrase, now converted into a Santi Pando mantra.

Cassio left just like he'd come in, without turning on a
light or leaving any trace. On JB Justo Avenue, the buildings howled above him. Saturn had wandered so close to the
southern hemisphere that its rings could be seen from human

soil with the naked eye, but the skies of Buenos Aires were clogged with huge piles of giant Angora cats. Cassio walked without seeing, his head down. He followed a well-known path: up Córdoba Avenue, then a perpendicular turn down the slope of Serrano. He went into a bar and sat down, his blue eyes hooded beneath the red lights, the lines of code printed on the floor tiles fading to null.

This was Mundo Bizarro, his favorite dive back in his peak hacking days. Here he had shared recreational beverages with the comrades who'd participated in that era's most renowned exploits. At the time, the computational elite was too self-sufficient to bother evangelizing in search of new recruits.

It was all so familiar: the Satanist kitsch and the toy psychodelia; the skinny woman who owned the place, and Piñata, the ancient bartender. At the far end of the bar sat the usual coke dealer. The air rang with the Cramps' "Cramps Stomp." And the screen that took up an entire wall was showing the original *Planet of the Apes*.

The battle-hardened apes gesticulated as if from outside a giant window; here inside, people moved their lips without creating meaning. There were people his age, about to summit the Everest of their cerebral power, perhaps wasting their synaptic lives as idiotically as he was. Most great mathematical discoveries burst up out of one's mental swamp before the age of twenty-five; now twenty-four, Cassio was already a veteran of the numbers wars, even if only he and the other members of his tiny brotherhood could still see them revarnished in glory there in the violet zones of the ample mind to which they all belonged. Cassio was hardly on the verge of seeing his name affixed to any cryptographic laws, and no one was breaking ground for any Brandão da Silva Square—he simply hadn't used his powers to do anything epic for society.

The past life of his mind distanced itself from him like an octopus, wriggling away behind a cloud of black ink. In a biography of Nikola Tesla—the only gift from his father that he still had—he'd read that *"the inventor is generally misunderstood and unrewarded. His true recognition lays in knowing that he belongs to an exceptionally gifted class, without which the human race would have lost a long time ago the fight against the elements."* He ordered a beer and a shot of Glenlivet, knew that his body wouldn't be able to take it, prepared himself for the numbness to come. He would let the alcohol oxidize his terminals, let his mind dwindle like some weary supernova collapsing into a blue or white dwarf star, millions of years condensed into a couple of hours (the human era on Earth) on his way to a serene depression that would leave him in bed for weeks.

A flash distracted him from his thoughts. The enormous eyes of the simians were staring at him. Several seconds passed. Now he blinked. Tall, blue eyes, elongated facial features: it was Max Lambard, illuminated by the LEDs.

Cassio remembered each and every detail of each and every time he'd seen Max, and everywhere he'd heard that Max had been. The first time, at MendozaConch, a hackers' conference in a bar on the corner of Maure and Luis María Campos, when Cassio was barely a human fungus, maybe thirteen years old. Max and his minions had formed TLO, Tetrakis Legomenon, the group responsible for some of the most distinguished cataclysms of the 1990s. Countless strikes from the shadows had been attributed to them, but they'd never been caught—they were a legend of sorts. That night, watching the TCP/IP championship, Cassio hadn't been able to talk himself into joining the competition, but he had tried tequila for the first time. The resulting state of emotional catatonia took him by surprise.

The members of TLO controlled parts of Satanic Brain, but in the outside world they maintained the strict anonymity befitting such an elite organization; only inferior entities were traceable, legible, vulnerable to law enforcement mendacity. They were a few years older than Cassio, thought of his group (DAN, Digital Anarchy) as upstart insects, referred to them as "Digging Anally." Compelled by hatred, DAN tried to hack Satanic Brain and take control of the TLO computers, with no demonstrable success. TLO's response to DAN's trench warfare was impermeable disdain. Later, in the Exact Sciences department, Max (who studied physics and biology for a couple of years before dropping out) had beat him at Ping-Pong several times. Cassio had never dared to reveal his identity. He'd wanted to think that Max Lambard knew exactly who he was, that his previous contempt was just a juvenile phase of a more omniscient, universal esprit de corps.

In fact, they'd only talked once, at a Defcon after-party back in 1999 or so. That year, Cassio and Luck had won two combat series: "Core Wars," where programs fight one another for control of a computer called MARS, and "Capture the Flag," the military strategy classic—their trophies were shards of a chip from Defcon's main console. That night,

Cassio and Luck had worn the fluorescent shards on lanyards, walking around the party and savoring the status that those splinters of the conference conferred in the eyes of their peers. It was the peak of all known glory—this was before the Defcon pool parties started filling with girls in bikinis and other identifiably female beings. The Argentine hackers all met up, drank beer with Canadians, Slovaks, Russians, and Yankees from both coasts. The global context and the end of the millennium had brought the many different hacker races together in this same melting pot, and peace was sealed between the legendary TLO and the triumphant DAN.

Max was there with Wari, who wore a T-shirt bearing the SSH intrusion code, and Riccardo, who had blue hair. Cassio remembered their conversation word for word: *Code is law, because code determines conduct, but what happens if we start writing code that we're incapable of reading? Algorithms are like a new adaptive species, a breed that is potentially superior to all others, because they acquire the form of truth very quickly, and blend themselves in with it. They are both the medium and the message, perhaps comparable, in terms of overwhelming power and attributed virtues, to the written word in the Biblical past. They are capable of becoming more and more real, reaching a point where they govern the reality of others. But if they've been designed and executed with sufficient brilliance, it's only fair that they be allowed to live independent lives.*

At that point the conversation was derailed, shifting to tasteless jokes about abortion and made-up profiles of future eco-activists who support the right to algorithmic life. Then it dissolved altogether. A few meters away, some hired girls were dancing with Hula-Hoops.

The following day, Cassio and Max ran into each other in the Defcon hallways. Max was wearing a *Blade Runner* T-shirt, and as it happened they were both crazy about the final scene, Rutger Hauer contemplating the destruction of his world. Cassio mentioned that the actor himself had improvised those lines; he was pleased to learn that Max hadn't known this.

Max's face is rather inexpressive, except for his big blue eyes, which bulge slightly, and can turn on or off according to the dictates of shadowy internal processes. Theories about his recent whereabouts had circulated unevenly: that he had moved to Burma; that he'd married an exotic dancer; that after a dose of ayahuasca he'd gone years without speaking to anyone, then begun communicating exclusively through numbers. That he'd made money in derivatives during the banking crisis and had gone to Thailand to get paid, but it turned out that he didn't like the beach, or at least not as much as he had thought, and that around that same time he'd taken up a strain of libertarianism, that sought to configure a better world for workers outside the system of nation-states, with offshore platforms beyond the reach of tax authorities and centuries-old laws; that he had been working on neuronal simulations in nematodes, and that his first incursions into biology had taken place in an unsterilized garage in the Villa Urquiza neighborhood of Buenos Aires. It was also rumored that he had millions of dollars' worth of stock options (hence his interest in avoiding the tax authorities), and that he had begun building certain machines, both theoretical and practical, in order to "test a few things."

And now Max seemed to remember something:

"Are you still working with *viri*?"

"No, I quit building viruses a while ago."

"It got too simple."

"Yeah, something like that. The structure is fairly trivial. Sometimes I get the feeling that the world hasn't fallen apart just because it has too many good people. At this point, systemic noncollapse can only be explained by postulating an ethical majority working in defense of the species."

"Ha, yeah, that's a good theory. What are you up to these days?"

Cassio tried to dodge the question, drowning it in his shot of single malt, but he ended up telling Max about his abandoned thesis, his incursion into the working world, Ship.e.bo. It was like a documentary of some recent war—his life as an arsenal of resources gone to waste, the hills of possibility now buried in fog. It had been a while since he'd had a *personal* conversation with anyone: his overexcitement spoke for him. In the end, he talked about everything except Melina.

Max listened attentively, sipping his beer. Two girls dressed in lace bodices climbed up on the bar to do an erotic dance. It was a fairly soft-core affair, done almost as a joke—they were friends of the house.

"One and zeroes, holes and poles," said Max.

He'd spoken somberly, now turned to Cassio, talked as if through a dreamlike mist.

"There was a time when we were navigating unexplored

areas in the dark, but we had instruments that were better than maps, and the owners of those spaces didn't even know they existed *as spaces*, much less how to find the access tunnels. For us it was like taking a stroll. And every human rite of intelligence is based on the same thing, on bonfires in the darkness, because nobody ever really knows . . . but now, no matter where you go, the sun's right there like some surgical lamp. People have decided that they want pre-industrial values, village life, the epiphanies of diets that reawaken the Neanderthal inside . . . An interconnected set of beings, an emerging society in need of new ways to adapt to the world. But the most interesting thing is that they've already decided that computers—and the software that is their blood—can perfectly well be combined with their own human bodies."

The conversation soon spilled over into personal research projects. Max was fascinated by informational processes in living tissue, with theories and applications that Cassio had never even heard of. He told Cassio about the latest analytical approaches to mitochondria, new theories about change and mutation that had been left out in the cold by both classic and modern Darwinism: namely, that mitochondria may have originated when a type of virus first attached itself to certain simple organisms, turning them into machines capable of metabolization and storage. And as for how certain processes originally began—say, photosynthesis—there was talk of early forms of retrovirus infecting a population of prehistoric algae. Chloroplasts capable of metabolizing the products of photosynthesis might well be the result of those ancient molecular invasions. In sum, an organism was invaded, and all the cells who failed to enter into a pact of submission with the invaders would die. The only successful population was that which internalized the virus, bowing to the invader and incorporating its DNA; the invading virus lived on inside the organism in all-but-invisible traces, without ever abandoning its own genetic load.

Cassio watched Max talk, every movement he made; his nausea had been replaced by another sort of dizziness, one that bordered on euphoria. He was participating in a personal conversation, and yet somehow it felt entirely natural. Now Max hummed as he fiddled with his glass, his voice vaguely metallic. He signaled to the bartender, ordered a cheeseburger. In the red glints of light, his face was clear and precise.

"All the scientific fields with exponential capacity have reached a point where they can no longer be regulated. True technology can never be fully regulated. When an elite trades on the future, it's her responsibility to move the edge of time, so that the others can never catch up. Which is why it's ridiculous to follow the rules rather than break things apart, to pay homage to hierarchies that no longer matter . . . I mean, they don't matter because they don't exist. They are *literally* inextant. It's as if they resided in another dimension, one that has no point of contact with the world of real technology."

Max's glass floated there on the bar in front of his nose, half its base resting on empty air. He peeled the damp label off of his beer bottle, stuck it beside the glass, and Cassio imagined a multidimensional surface that ran through everything, that moved about in absolute space; he felt it spin, turning in circles around him, beams of dark matter bearing it unstably. He didn't know what he thought anymore, and didn't catch the beginning of Max's next sentence, but even more powerful than his intuitional visions was the feeling that the music of Max's argument was approaching its logical conclusion.

The little erotic dance was over, and the two girls were now French kissing; a few people came up, applauded, ordered more drinks. Max set his empty bottle on the edge of the bar and carried on. Strictly speaking, he said, *all of them* were witnesses to what was going on. Everything on the web devoted to entertaining us, it was all just the festive phase of the bellicose as absorbed by the social. The renovation of the military-industrial complex consisted of this mix of entertainment, espionage and civilian lives entangled as friends and enemies. In fact, it couldn't even really be said that what programmers built was technology—the challenges that most Web-based endeavors dealt with consisted in making things ever easier, simpler, making their use ever more trivial.

A fresh beer appeared on the bar, a movement so quick it seemed agent-less. Max shrugged.

"Of course . . . there's nothing wrong with all that. It's not like I'm saying the apps are stupid. I mean, *of course* they're stupid, but that's not the point . . . The point is that the whole thing is a bit too soft for the type of human the species needs. The target just offers itself up for dissection, puts sensors all over itself—the products it consumes, the spaces it chooses to inhabit . . . The white empire dedicates itself to whitening the world until everything is completely transparent. And the ones that used to be on our side are now our enemies . . .

The arrival of the hamburger extended the ellipsis. Cassio prayed that Max wouldn't say it, wouldn't *pronounce* it out loud, because he'd already made it clear: Cassio had chosen a life that was an insult to his brain, to the homunculus in whose true heart resides the vital notion of dignity. The drinks were no longer wetting his throat—it felt like he was suffocating. Max let mayonnaise drip methodically onto his plate beside his French fries ("Honestly, mayonnaise is intolerable except in the company of potatoes"), and after a few large, calm bites, he continued:

"It's as if no one really understands what's happening or what's at stake"—he lowered his voice—"when you're dealing with technology designed to transfer and analyze information on a level and scale that can't be replicated any other way. There's a race going on between technology and politics, and it's obvious which side is best equipped to win."

He couldn't say much more about the Project, not yet, but it was clear to Cassio that Max was in command of some new technology that was both exciting and entirely unknown to the rest of the world. Cassio wasn't used to working with live tissue, but from an engineerable perspective, the Project opened up a unique research space, with a quantum leap's worth of advantage over other analytical ventures. In Max's words, it "could redefine all existing relationships with infor-mation."

He had convinced the Balseiro Institute, which was part of the Bariloche Atomic Center down in Patagonia, to let him use their laboratory. Balseiro owned a very small stake in Max's company, had no real veto power on the board, but their involvement was helping to accelerate the whole process. He admitted that what he really wanted was to set up his own lab. It was crazy to have to depend on the university system or the state; he'd rather associate himself with some sadistic idiot, though that was basically the same thing. Serious technology should be built somewhere free of all outside demands, he said, so that innovative potential was the only thing determining what made it into the portfolio of priorities.

Max broke off, began humming, tried to peel the label off his latest bottle. This one didn't come off so easily. Cassio understood perfectly. Max had had to move fast, which is why he'd cut a deal with the center—there was no need to justify anything.

"We've got an advantage of a year or two, no more. The odds are bad. But it's possible."

They kept talking until the bar closed, then walked through the dark streets to El Galeón, a place down on Santa Fe y Gurruchaga that was open all night. When they parted ways at seven A.M., the doormen were out washing down the sidewalks. It had been a while since Cassio had last seen a sunrise or smelled the odor of damp clothing that results from alcohol in the blood dehydrating the brain. A very light breeze parted his bangs, one final whisper of fresh air; the solid heat of summer was gathering force above the city, and its arrival was imminent. A subterranean current of new blood was flowing beneath the asphalt. In the early light, objects seemed to be covered by a sticky patina, as if the terrors of the world had been appeased, sprinkled with color, and brought back to life just for him.

His sense of unease had completely disappeared; he felt lucid, at peace. When he entered his room, Harpo the turtle lifted his snout; lately his movements had slowed considerably. Cassio caressed the glass and emptied a little packet of food into the morbid water. He knew that little turtles didn't live very long. He couldn't take Harpo to Bariloche—the laws of the province prohibited the entry of foreign pets. He imagined a greenish cloud of tiny turtles rising above the rocky shore of Lago Gutiérrez, finding new life in the nearby trees. Harpo swam a little, then floated in place, hovering there in the water. Maybe Cassio could take him as contraband, put him in a plastic tube like the ones architects use to transport their blueprints.

He closed the blinds in his room, leaving it completely dark. He took off his socks and lay down on his bed. From the far end of the bed, his toes appeared to be looking at him, awaiting a reaction on his part. He took up his laptop, opened it on his chest, and bought a one-way airplane ticket to Bariloche.

Cassio took charge of organizing the research group. Focusing on a new passion infused his body with the tension of well-being: the challenges were vast and complex, right at the level of his neural ambition. The fact that the technology's potential hazards were still impossible to quantify—these were new, violent, devastatingly specialized techniques for approaching the data—made the job feel like a return to the simple and beautiful things life had to offer, things that didn't require intricate abilities such as talking to people, participating in society, or smiling.

He'd arrived alone in Bariloche. Located near the southern end of the continent, surrounded by mountains and the blue mirrors of water, it had been the destination of choice for his earliest camping trips with his brotherhood of nerds. Cassio had spent the best summers of his life pushing deep into the swamps, advancing through the silvery conifers, swimming in cobalt-blue lakes, being eaten alive by horseflies, and taking respectful ownership of the immensity like some creature from Tolkien. Back then, everyone wore bermuda shorts, and no one shaved or cut their hair. Bariloche was a male arcadia bustling with sports—snowboarding, rock climbing—that he aspired to learn. Here were his most highly valued memories, his moments in the shadow of a shining, distinctly masculine life: striking out, fishing for trout in the lakes, offering soliloquies to the mountains, and investigating the darkest corners of his mind—the best ecstasy dealer he'd ever known.

And now he was working at the Balseiro Institute. If he

hadn't fallen under the Venusian spell of cryptography, he would have loved to study here. The fact that his lab belonged to the Balseiro was for him a hero's badge: Balseiro was the closest to a romantic dream of academic life, but the fact that he was here to work on a secret disruptive technology project was the cherry icing on the nerd cake.

In certain places, the sky above the mountain range makes itself absolute, the clouds brushing against one's very throat. Even Cassio could feel these sensations, and he'd developed a childlike ability to appreciate them. He rented a little apartment on Onelli Street, a block from the waterfront; from his armchair he could see Nahuel Huapi Lake stretching out like a languid blue animal. Eventually, he stopped thinking about Melina, though every so often he used her to boot up violent, abstract, haughty spasms in the shower. He decorated his room with a limited-edition poster of Chewbacca heading into the forest with his bandoliers of ammunition and his AK-47, a rousing portrait of the formerly tame beast that would accompany him from now until the multimillion-dollar sale of the company.

In principle, Niklas Bruun's life has unfolded on its own terms. Initiated into his chosen science at an early age, his ventures into society occurred only in moments of necessity, his nervous system brushing more or less unexpectedly against the real world. A ground-skimming heir to tradition, he displays the innovative nature of those who excavate fundamental betrayals hidden amidst known feats of daring. His writing strikes a solitary tone; during the period in question, the words he writes are meant never to be read.

His journal entries are interspersed with sketches of creatures drawn from nature. There are images of extraordinary flowers, and elliptical chronicles of insects seen in the course of his voyages. At the time, however, there are never any *people* present in his journal, nothing that would imply any personal relationships.

According to the pens of his critics, the biographical record of Niklas's mental life appears and disappears like a snake crawling through bushes. Though the thicket covers three continents in all, for a time there is only one. Niklas in Amsterdam, a vagabond, intoxicated on a blend of absinthe and *frica* (a first reference to the presence of the Tupinambá elixir in Europe). Niklas amidst crevices of cerulean ice, on a trip to collect purple orchids and lichen for a Slavic collector of whom no one had ever heard. Niklas arguing in a half-empty conference room in Madrid; Niklas in Lapland, stretching out a cold-numbed hand to draw; Niklas hurrying out of the Lusitano palace, having refused to discuss anything that wasn't hyperborean insects.

In his journal, he explains that the plants he draws seem to him to be "a reorganization of human eyes—of the entire human face." His writings begin to fill with descriptions of strange specimens, ones that future naturalists will be unable to connect to extant vegetal species in any way *outside of his journal*; in the course of his nocturnal raptures (accompanied by his favorite apéritif, Valdemar, a bit spilled on the page), he comes to believe that he discovered these creatures in his dreams, where he has seen himself moving through underwater caverns, arriving at deranged islands where he is welcomed by mysterious breezes and ground-level clouds not found anywhere else in his writings. "The pools of black gall that await deep in the secret swamps preserve the most extravagant of species: excrescences that suddenly cease their crawling behavior and appear to become a motionless vegetal species, waiting to be ingested providentially, and once made part of the internal environment of their host, they regain their animal form; in this magnificent, fearless kingdom, unimaginable kinships are formed between one species and another . . ." Bruun dissects, composes small portraits; on nights when he is inspired, he works on his ode to *Numidae Espora*. And then we lose all track of him.

Most likely he is off collecting specimens for Tartare d'Hunval, penetrating the Amazon in a series of ten-day expeditions, returning each time bearing treasure in the form of new species.

Do you think that it's alive? You would be surprised. The path of these plants runs between life and death; they aren't of the world of the living, but it can't be said that they have passed on . . . As you will see, they react furiously to the slightest of stimuli. Their appearance sometimes seems to indicate a putrefactive form, closely allied to fungi and other such beings . . . Their very nature leads them to the limits of their organizationless existence, and from that existential floor they lash out against their enemies. Do you see, do you realize what I'm saying?

His earliest contact with Tartare was related to a series of *Crissia pallida* specimens, which Tartare had obtained by calling in favors from his network of botanical spies. Tartare claimed that he was simply attracted to the beautiful, simple, black profundity of botany itself, but the tenor of Niklas's research changed radically after he met Tartare. They were united by their passion for *Crissia*, and for the study of beings that are born and die outside the realm of all that we think of as real.

Like two ears connected by a wrinkled labellum: the bridge where the insects are lost. As if already condemned to death, they cross it in a state of stupefaction. Libidinous cavern, a paradise created for the depraved, the site induces changes within their bodies.

Tartare set his eyeglasses aside; they were damp with tears. Niklas stayed focused on the magnificent pearlescent creature, which seemed drawn from some epic he'd never read.

When the foot merged with the head, the labellum applied pressure to the sac, which began to fill with succulent aromas, and

*the axis was inverted: the root was now drawn toward the
light of the sun, while a few late-growing bulbs remained
near the rock that served as horizon, as watershed. Farther
down, the two extremely white and meaty flowers defied
architectural norms by growing toward the ground, bur-
rowing down through the air, still bearing the now half-dead
insects they had drugged.* Sero te amavi, *Crissia.*

As for Tartare: it had been a malodorous, gelatinous caterpillar, *Phobetron pithecium dhunvalica*, native
to the swamps of Madagascar, that had launched his
scientific reputation. He had spent several months
admiring them there in the mud; had led them
gently into his glass bottles, had sunk into the muck
with them, had observed them talking to him in his
dreams. He had proposed the first scientific description of the caterpillar, removing it from its originary
swamp, binding it to his lineage.

Years later, deep in the Mongolian forest, Tartare had
gone blind for several days, which he spent entrapped
in the (quite reasonable) belief that he was going to die.
For context: in that jungle lives a termite whose man-
dibles are so powerful that their workings are audible
to the human ear. Back when Tartare's powerful footfall
was first heard in the zone, no one had ever heard of
Nubia crisallis, and no one could have predicted the
means by which the spore made its way into one's
brain. It had entered through his ear, made a pilgrimage
through the inner passageways of consciousness much
like a memory as described by St. Augustine, and finally

reached the cerebral meat of its host. When Tartare returned to Amsterdam, he was unrecognizable.

He claimed that he had been possessed by a series of intuitions that were "completely foreign to the manner in which I had conceived the world," as he would put it in his new book. Not only had he changed externally; his entire being was imbued with new vigor. He was sure that evolution *à la Darwinienne* was on its last legs, and in the new classification system that he was designing, certain species fit inside others; they invaded one another, arriving at a matrix of forms that couldn't be reduced to the issue of mere survival, much less that of *generations* (an idea he found repugnant). Evolutionary change, he believed, happened much more quickly—within the lifespan of a single individual. Rather than waiting for reproductive cycles to silently select useful features, it occurred via mimesis, and as the result of unexpected contact.

Tartare opened his house there in Amsterdam to a series of scientific spiritualism sessions—trances in which the participants claimed to travel through different geological eras. At these parties, there was a medium who helped the invitees fall into reveries (encouraged by the ingestion of *frica*) that led them from the dawn of the Devonian to the migrations of the Cretaceous. Niklas would have taken part in these ceremonies.

As Torben Schatts comments in his memoirs, "Everything about [Tartare] denotes a highly refined man irremediably corrupted by his frequenting of actresses, ballerinas, and *frica*." In fact, at the time Tartare had decided to content his appetites with nothing but writing and thought. He had promised himself that he would remain celibate until his next book, *Orchidaceaen Dithyrambs*, was published. In that text he portrays this stretch of his life as follows:

No longer was I that timorous man of yesteryear, the one who stammered the Latin names of the kingdoms under his breath. No longer was I content to hide away amidst my magnificent collection, which was already wholly known to me, and yet through which whole tomes of future natural history could be written. Disdain had given me a second skin, one that was impervious to the digressions of others. It no longer gave me any pleasure merely to crush their meager insights with my perfect erudition; I was ready to destroy their egos altogether with my nomenclaturical euphoria, much the way collapsing towers of stone will squash men like insects.

His *Monographie des Termiten* was one of the first works to be labeled "speculative botany." It circulated amongst whispers, accumulating intriguing silences ("culebrin attacks," in the words of Tartare) and raised eyebrows from those who were capable of raising them. He would later write that snares had already been set with him in mind, and indeed, the judgment of *naturalia* expert Giovanni Savonarola, creator and destroyer of naturalist reputations, was not long in coming:

The naturalist T. d'Hunval doubtless possesses a talent beyond the ordinary, but he exaggerates his stature as a man of science, and lacks any sense of criteria or rigor . . . and the same can be said of his Monographie. *The divine language of Theophrastus as he presented the new field of study at Plato's academy, and that of Linnaeus when he transformed the field to address secular*

needs, suffers cruel distortions in the hands of d'Hunval,
ones that are frankly quite difficult to tolerate. One is
reminded of Friedrich Vischer, who held that there were
paintings whose stench one could actually see. Tartare
d'Hunval's book presents us with the horrifying notion
that there are scientific compositions whose stinking breath
one can actually touch. His naturalist legacy will likely be
comparable to the lives of certain insects, best summarized
as "a quick trip to the surface before sinking once more
into the swamp."

And then "the abyss, the abominable nothing, phan-
toms spilling over my name, over me" (*Orchidaceaen
Dithyrambs*, 45). Tartare d'Hunval tries to console himself with thoughts of his destiny as a scientific martyr,
and a possible life for his text as an obscure classic. He
walks along the Herengracht in Amsterdam feeling like
a haloed ghost, intimately protected by his intuitions,
his unique visions of caterpillars having slough-bound
love affairs with termites and orchids; he talks to himself
out loud, tells himself that the only thing that matters
is the truth. The aquatic labyrinth of the city leads
him from euphoria to melancholy. Much like his caterpillars, he forms a close relationship with muddy
water, though these swamps are only infested with
humans; he is almost invisible within the walled-in
underworld he inhabits. And he can no longer stand
the city. In his journal he notes, "*Incomparabilis nocta
. . . Nictabo splendens*," and draws the profile of a flower
that is an insect, its wings outspread.

Numbed by the indifference to his work, Tartare abandons all formal links to the scientific community of his time. He moves to Rio de Janeiro, capital of the Empire of Brazil, later writing that he'd "wanted to be devoured by pure, hard research." This is the prelude to his most awe-inspiring project, and to the very night that brings us back into contact with Niklas Bruun and the vertigo he feels when in touch with "impure science," as he calls the dark constellations working their way into the history of science of the Anthropocene.

Upon arriving in Rio de Janeiro, Tartare acquires an old Jesuit church which had been abandoned when the Companhia de Jesus was exiled from Brazil. The vegetation had done its work: the oblong sacristy had become a terrarium, its glass and adobe enclosing pure jungle. Like the tails of gigantic monkeys, vines brushed against the floor where Communion had once been given. The building was a perfect symbol for the challenges of faith in a place where everything up to and including God is eaten by some greater power, and it was precisely what Tartare was looking for. He hired a local man named Zizinho and began construction.

He knocked down the walls of the naves and installed iron staircases connected by hanging walkways that formed a tightening spiral as they climbed. He crowned what was left of the ceiling with a cupola of glass panes and long iron tentacles. To those with a view of Monte da Conceição's haughty profile, the cupola looked like a gigantic insect, an exquisite tarantula mounted beneath the constellations of the Southern Hemisphere, where there is always more darkness than stars.

Inside his jungle greenhouse, Tartare installed fans to simulate a breeze; the blades combed softly through the layers of plants that grew on the balconies, including worm-infested phosphoric palms from the kingdom of Surinam that sprayed their amber light throughout the tarantula's interior. Along the walls, a majestic variety of vegetal species "amenable to experimentation" (op. cit.) grew into a labyrinth of leafy waterfalls that replicated themselves via mirrors strategically placed in each cul-de-sac and along dead-end walkways, augmenting the overall effect. Zizinho bought a pig's stomach, built a bellows to serve as fumigator and pollinator, filled it with cyanide compounds and pollen. The two pet rabbits, Plato and Aristotle, who'd come with Tartare from Holland, began to leave clumps of fur all over, until one day they were found dead. Before burning the bodies, Tartare removed the fat and used it to fertilize his vegetal creatures; they reacted by growing lushly, as if the poisoned tissue of the mammals were the very breath of life.

Each evening around sunset, guests began to arrive. Among the collectors were Bateson from England, the entomologists Arielus Languis and Karl Stu, Kasia Melerina and Baron Tel, Barbosa-Lenz, and Nunzia Lucrezia Damátida, in whose reddish hair was an ornament made of *Scorpioniadie scintillans*, a translucid scorpion with golden legs. Venetia d'Adda made an entrance: swathes of tulle in black and blue and green, a tall beehive hairdo, a shoulder-length mantilla bearing pieces of jewelry in the shape of fruits, beetles and tiny luminescent

worms. Tartare mentioned "Emperor Dom João and the unidentified women from the courtesan world who accompany him, each wearing a hairpiece of dried snakes, each with thin gold chains coiled around her arms." Zizinho, dressed in his dinner jacket, offers every new arrival a glass overflowing with sparkling *salep*, a medieval cocktail based in orchid juices, and garnished with a twist of *Spilanthes oleracea*, an herb that produces an electric-eel tingling on the tongue.

One night the guests were led to what was once the sacristy, rebuilt as an august cabinet room in fine hardwoods. Inside the glass cases were mummified arthropods, several herbolaria, and a map of the stars made of insects, their carapaces diffracting the light. There was the strong smell of formaldehyde, made even stronger by the heat. The guests—resplendent in their tulle gowns, tuxedos, kid-leather shoes—barely fit into the space between the wooden cabinets and the species on display. The smell grew more and more dense, and a woman fell to the floor, unconscious. Tartare exults in his notes: "Only extreme naïveté could lead anyone to think the altar a work of improvisation. And a velvet mantle covers the secret . . . perhaps a glass chest holding some new species?"

As he also notes, "I later learned that he was there . . . blending in with the others, seemingly just another guest." The identity of this mysterious visitor would not be revealed until sometime later, but it was on that very night, according to Tartare's diary, that he first heard of Hoichi's garden. The resulting voyages would lead him deep into the jungle.

Tartare made a small bow toward his guests, and lifted his glass. He held it in the air for several seconds, then looked at Zizinho. Solemnly, Zizinho pulled back the blue velvet mantle, revealing a glass chest with an intricate frame of wood and silver. He opened the lid. Then Tartare bent over with a smile and blew.

Chaos reigned that night. Tartare's glass chest made prisoners of them all. No one knew if its contents were samples of a new species that no one had ever heard of, or an isolated experiment whose chemical workings they couldn't begin to imagine. The entire salon went mad. Niklas remembers the event as follows:

Inside were flowers with hooded blooms, like cloistered Franciscan monks in the act of meditation. The humble bouquet contrasted stridently with the preceding orchidacean magic, with the cabinetry, the expectations, and above all with the combined egos of Venetia d'Adda and Tartare d'Hunval. What occurred next is reserved exclusively to the New World memories of those present. As Tartare blew into the chest, a very dense golden powder surged from tiny brown holes in the blossoms. The powder rose up through the gathered guests, navigated through the air overhead in a sinusoid of gold. On the verge of losing consciousness, the guests stretched out their necks to breathe in mouthfuls of this wonder. Then the hallucinations began: it seemed to me that we walked for hours through pastures and along strips of marsh that stretched out like tunnels through the jungle. At certain moments, the color green filled my eyes, I couldn't make out shapes of any kind, and I felt a taste at once bitter and sweet, a fleck of swamp voyaging through my mouth. But there is one thing I can be sure of. I saw blackish worms take position on the outstretched arm of a young woman, saw them bury themselves in her veins, watched them disappear into pure white foam. She shuddered, opened her eyes wide as the beings mixed with her blood. I tried to approach her, felt that I had to talk to her.

Amidst other spoils of that night, Tartare received a series of offers for the chest—ten thin natives, a number of native children, a medieval castle built just for him in the middle of the Parà jungle. Biting back a faint smile, without saying a word Tartare slipped through the crowd and disappeared through a hidden door, leaving a wake of tulle and glints of light. Zizinho was left with the task of turning away the potential buyers.

Intuiting, perhaps, that the world as he knew it had come to an end, Niklas drew strange translucid plants in his journal, and beneath them he wrote, *Hic captabis frigus opacum (here I found the fresh darkness)*. In the morning, a hungover and half-dressed Tartare came looking for him. The glass chest had disappeared. The plants stared at Niklas, mute.

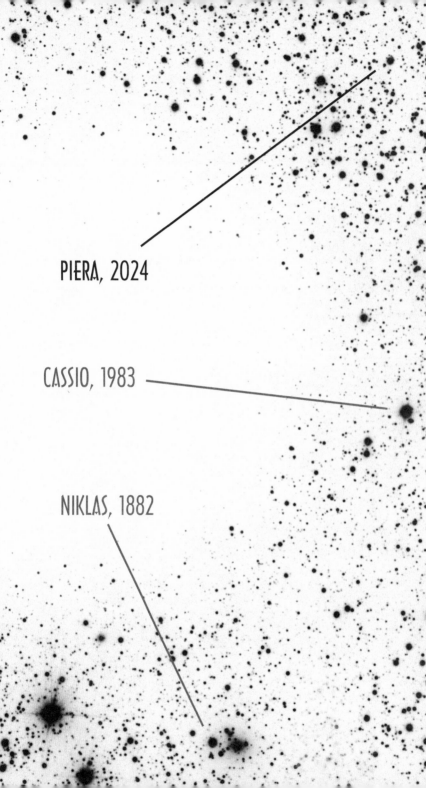

PIERA, 2024

CASSIO, 1983

NIKLAS, 1882

The key to successful technology consists of convincing addicts that the future's heart beats within it, that its mere existence entails the inexorable dissolution of their enemies. In principle, its users are born different from one another, but soon they begin to resemble one another so much that in the end they cease to exist as individuals. Only by collaborating with the invasion can they survive.

In the laboratory lobby, a black flag with a pirate insignia stretches across a wall; beneath the skull are the words COMMITMENT TO EXCELLENCE in red letters. Grouped together on an island in the center, computers are stacked like geological strata. There are various panels and metal frames at varying levels of plenitude and disintegration; there are mathematical functions written in green and blue on a whiteboard, monitors and other apparati on the floor, a white camera hanging from the center of the ceiling. High on a rack, rock-climbing shoes ooze with faint intimations of rotting dairy products. Out the massive window, Andean foothills descend to a turquoise lake and the concrete cubes of the Project; it looks like an architect's model, mountain and metal and cement scripted with shadows. Cassio would later learn that Max Lampard had filled the office/lab with furniture he'd found in the warehouses of the Institute and the center.

Two heads lift, disoriented, as if they've smelled something strange. The recent arrival's hand rises machine-like, a vaguely robotic flag of empathy.

"I'm Piera," she says. "How's it going?"

They continue to look at her. Small of stature, no lab coat, dark hair with a few blue strands—the boys of the Project must think she's on the administrative staff, here to look for something that's gone missing. Piera knows these moments well, and enjoys the incredulity. She suppresses a yawn. Talking just makes her want to yawn sometimes.

She had seen several films of the group at work; they'd been sent to "accelerate the integration process." Vignettes of her future colleagues, several hundred hours time-lapsed into a hundred hours of footage. It was recommended that she play it while working or otherwise busy with other things, not really paying attention, so as to get used to being close to them both physically and mentally. When she arrived in Bariloche, Piera turned on the heating, got into bed wearing all of her sweaters at once, and watched the video at x8. The frenetic motion was funny with the volume off.

She also had a look at the employee files. Fredy, twenty-four, Belgian, electronic engineer. Rama, twenty-three, beard, a surprisingly high IQ for a mechanical engineer: for some reason he reminded her of a mentally deficient albino that she'd met in Montevideo. Riccardo, the guru sidekick, Max Lambard's main partner, who moves about the room like a rising prince of technology. Pablo, twenty-seven, working on genetic interface, talks all the time, barely moves his eyebrows.

Piera put the video back on normal speed and turned up the volume. Pablo separated his speeches with the phrase "Is that clear?" which appeared to irritate the others. She decided that she liked him a lot, and lit a joint, some

Paraguayan bud that had passed through the scanners without a problem. She focused on the Kanban board and its little colored papers defining the tasks to be done. This was the Japanese organizational tool that took Toyota to its peak in the 1980s; the Americans had absorbed it into their MBA programs. She whistled a few times as she read through the tasks, but getting things done ahead of time wasn't the idea. The team's beings were more entertaining than their work, and now it was Cassio's turn—big guy, hair like buckwheat. Apparently he didn't talk much—in general it was the others talking to him. Piera took a drag and closed her eyes, followed the meditation instructions she'd learned in San Francisco. Her mind produced the image of soft cheeses stacked like a snowman. She let herself doze off.

It had been a while since she'd worked with Argentinians; the idea sounded like fun. She knew that, like all human groups, eventually they would stop sniffing around her as if she were some foreign object, would come to perceive her as a *person*. At some point (and Piera loved this point), everyone was reduced to a molecular sketch of themselves, a minimal quantum of personality. And she'd decided some time ago that being a person didn't actually make her feel anxious.

"You got here! Wow, I think you're the first living being to figure out how to find this place on your own. Welcome!"

It was Max. They'd met on Skype; he was taller and a little better looking than she'd thought. He gave her a brief hug—manly, transmitting a sense of protection—and carried on talking as he turned to the rest:

"Hey everybody. Hey! *Achtung*, babies. This is Piera, our star biologist. Piera, this is our humble Stromatoliton research group. Like I already told you all, Piera is a genius. Piera, I hope you'll be comfortable here. If it's okay with you, this desk here can be yours, and you've got your own spot in the clean room—Cassio will show it to you. Right now everybody's hard at work, so we'll put off the individual introductions for a bit, but I want you to get to know the charms of each member of this extremely charming group."

Heterosexual camaraderie is an extremely thin parabola. In this particular field, the idea persisted that the appearance of women was a preamble to decline—that the presence of girls was a signal that the revolutionary period of a company had ended, or was beginning to end. It signified that the *normal* period was starting, full of unmarried females and middle management, i.e., mediocrity.

Piera smiled without showing her teeth. It was important to let the jokes run their own benign course, to attack only when it wouldn't seem defensive. Max Lambard leaned over a head that ended in a ponytail:

"Later you'll take her to Antares and get her properly drunk."

"Alcohol's not my thing," she said. "Just pure heroin, and eight-balls of crack."

Cheerful murmurs. Ice broken.

Max lowered his gaze to the little apparatus on his arm, and took his leave with a wink. The kid with the ponytail (Leni? Piera wasn't sure she'd seen him in the video) came walking up with his hand outstretched:

"Waskam. Leni Waskam," he said.

He held out a maté. Piera took it, smelled the infusion.

"It's mine, but I activated it for you so that our microbes can flow together in friendship."

Piera toasted him, took a sip, and the eyes of all present shone brightly as they watched.

Her last job had been at the main Bionose laboratory in San Francisco. There she'd studied under Otrayo, a Chilean-American hippie with a PhD in medicine, hired to help the employees' minds achieve psychomagical moments, to open themselves to the enchantment of existence. Piera closed her eyes and visualized currents of water pouring into the deep, pushed her thoughts toward pools that grew bluer and bluer; she was to do so until an unexpected image came to her, and for the next few minutes her mental life was to organize itself around this image. If she saw a boat, she made sentences with the boat—the boat just now turned on the heater, the boat had left its chewing gum in its jacket—until it no longer held her attention. It was kind of a dumb exercise, but after doing it, something in her brain became accessible once again, and she could return to programming clear-headed. Just now, however, magic events were taking place outside her actual window: an incomparable sunset, with golden striations streaking the sky, and clouds gliding about, a system of fiery ships. She got up to make herself some tea.

Stromatoliton had offered her Las Araucarias—a luxurious house on Nahuel Huapi, surrounded by araucaria pines and other conifers, reserved for special visitors—but Piera had declined. She didn't want to live on the lake, as it made her dream of seismic movements weaving back and forth beneath her, of nocturnal lakequakes. Moreover, a view of the *real* lake might interfere with her imaginary lake, might dismantle the visual entertainment she needed for cerebral relaxation. She described these fears endearingly, and they were accepted as a charming quirk.

The arrivals manager took for granted that Piera knew all about the recent cases of persons devoured on the lakeshore, and explained that both the police and the Ministry of Genetics were looking into them. No explanation had been needed. She was given a small apartment with big windows looking onto the mountain peaks, which resembled the knuckles of a fist raised against the sky. The apartment was located above a bakery, which Piera took to be an opening onto a happiness she'd never felt before—a life of freshly baked croissants for breakfast every morning. But beginning around four A.M. each morning, the constant hum of moving pistons rose up through her floor, which turned her insomnia (which was only the result of living somewhere new, though the others referred to it as "urban sleeplessness") into a vice.

She studied the sky for a time, sipping her rosehip tea until the darkness had covered everything. There were ten or so men on the Stromatoliton staff with whom she wouldn't have to work directly; some of them had something resembling a concrete masculine form. In general she appreciated the trait of manliness, but wasn't attracted to any of these particular beings.

According to what little she'd seen walking around the civic center, Bariloche was still a profoundly masculine world, thick with testosterone both indoors and out. The local demographic appeared to be composed first and foremost of an elite corps of engineers and scientists working in the hard sciences. They'd been drawn here by the city's reputation as the continent's preeminent science hub, rivaled only by the Manaus Industrial Zone in Brazil, the lab complex at the Federal University of Latin American Integration in Foz de Iguazú, and the Technological City in Iquitos, Peru, all of which were focused on south-to-south biotech swaps with China.

Another testosterone-rich group consisted of alpinists, skiers, and rock climbers summoned here by the resurgent paradise of high jungle, trout-filled streams, conifer forests, and countless lakes. Although these men hardly interacted with those of the other group, they all wore the same alpine outfits, which gave them all the same rural Patagonian air, which made them all look alike. This was something that Bariloche and San Francisco had in common: everyone was dressed for a triathlon, formalwear was casual (sports) wear, people probably bonded through extended periods of hiking together, which made it hard for the newcomers, who had everything to share except for mountain time spent together. According to one of Piera's personal theories, concentrated testosterone eventually dissolved individual masculine features; this could be observed on soccer teams, and in tech companies too. In her field of work, it was most clearly seen in the nerds who began to develop thin, high voices and notable mammary curves.

There were still a few colleagues left to inspect. Piera plugged in the flash drive that held the introductory video, and set her tea off to one side. Then she opened a darknet screen, which was configured so as to leave no trace of her visits. She put a piece of tape over the built-in camera in case anyone tried to spy on her (this happened fairly often) and went to YouSuXXX. She put on the special glasses and closed her eyes. Two Komodo dragons—black skin, iridescent stripes—were attacking a very thin blonde woman who was completely naked except for her white tennis shoes. Piera made a few gestures in the air; the blonde stood up on the bed and smiled at the dragons. The dragons slowly closed in; at times they had human faces and hands. By now the blonde had practically lost consciousness, and her hair was thick with sweat; there were black snakes hiding inside her, famished and feeding, coming out only to breathe. Piera began to masturbate, rubbing a stick of deodorant against the soft fabric of her underwear. After a time, the dragons' movements began to slow. They took turns squeezing the snakes out of the woman's anus; trembling, they worked to wring out more juice. White fluids dripped from the hole down the side of the bed to the carpet. Distracted, Piera noted the money shot, and thus the nearing conclusion; she moved the cursor back to the beginning.

Then a document on the flash drive caught her eye. She opened it, and at first glance she couldn't tell what it was, but it was handwritten, saved in digital form for posterity. It was signed by Max Lambard; the words looked like groups of hunched homunculi. It didn't fill the page the completely, the document broken on the screen, her broken brain. It was a *poem*. And it wasn't the only poem. Apparently he wrote poems periodically, whenever he felt inspired by the discreet pleasures of natural language. This one summarized the vision of the company in bullet points:

- *Every human action has consequences in physical space.*
- *Like the waves that a stone creates as it falls into a pond, the consequences of human actions spill out over the world. They are perceptible long after the stone has sunk.*
- *(If they did not have consequences, they could not aspire to be called actions, as it is indisputable that they would not be acting upon anything.)*
- *Millions of stones per second falling into a pond generate waves that intermingle, intersect, interfere with one another, much like the waves formed by meteorites raining into the primordial swamp.*
- *For someone watching the pond, it would be inconceivable to try to distinguish the effects of one particular stone amongst all the others.*
- *Attempting to reconstruct the precise location where each stone struck the water an instant ago would be likewise unthinkable.*
- *Nonetheless, what has occurred lives on in the pond. The actions of men live on in the space of the world as effects spilling out within a system. They survive their actors in time, and represent them.*
- *These are the fundamental principles of Stromatoliton, the fount of its knowledge and the origin of its power.*

Until that moment, most of what Piera knew about Stromatoliton—aside from the Kanban board and some photographs of Sector 4—came from graphic stories that occasionally flooded the media for months at a time. She also knew, thanks to a few of Max's comments during the interview process, that reverse engineering metabolic paths—her specialty—had a central role to play at the company. Now she saw that there were still other documents on the flash drive. Filmed materials on the history of Bariloche (originally Chilean territory), recommended restaurants, a mountain trail guide, the telephone numbers of some hiking lodges. She'd heard that Max encouraged these kinds of expeditions, that once a month he took off to spend the night at a hiking shelter high in the mountains. There were also maps of the labyrinth of tunnels that connected the underground site beneath the Balseiro Institute to Huemul Island, and of abandoned railroad tunnels that cut straight through the Andes.

Piera had taken the job in a rare upsurge of pro–Latin American sentiment that was strengthened by the fact that she was sick of San Francisco, and of life in the United States in general. According to her friends in the area, there was a difference between the burnouts, as they called the crack-addict zombies that turned circles in the Tenderloin near the hotel where she lived, and those who were simply poor. The poor were nothing but slag, because they didn't achieve what they should have, didn't work hard enough—they were traitors to the American dream, and as such an affront to the American

species. The burnouts, on the other hand, had chosen mar-
ginality, and thus liberty. In San Francisco itself, according
to her friends' arguments, there were no real poor people,
only burnouts.

In Piera's opinion, living in a place where you could fall to
the ground half-dead and no hospital would treat if you if you
didn't have the money to pay for it was the very definition of
hell, of systemic disdain for humanity. Soon, she would start
to see the cool bohemian past of the city as a cautionary tale
of the pointlessness of American liberals. Despite the young
talent connected to the area, it was a fairly conservative place:
personal enjoyment was not a relevant endeavor, and those
who pretended to seek it moved to LA. As for the rest of it, in
the United States, technology had entered too quickly into its
normal phase, in the Kuhnian sense: given the constant evolution of laws that sought to encircle it, technology was no
longer free to continue developing. Regulation killed the
fun, the experimentation. The lawyers and the innovators
were both predators, competing with one another for the
right to transform their shared territory. The biological
cycle of technology required a different type of ecosystem
altogether. (Piera didn't think of Google as real technology,
of course—it was more an excuse for regulation, and its
rate of innovation was far too low given its potential.) It
was Piera's deeply rooted belief (deduced from a luminous
paragraph in *Neuromancer*—she thought of Gibson as her
guru scribe) that for technology to develop in all its splendor,
it must do so in a context of anarchy, with as little regulation as
possible. This was never going to happen in the United States.

The Stromatoliton proposal intrigued her enough that although the setup looked for all the world like a subsidiary of a state-run organization, she agreed to work with Max in spite of her principles. The digital spy scandals in Germany, Brazil, and Bolivia had accelerated her decision. The Regional Reorganization Plan enabled Latin American governments to decline the services of American megacorporations subject to the Patriot Act and thus required to surrender user information (genetic and otherwise) every time an agency with a three-letter acronym requested it. The Workers' Party in Brazil had taken the initiative by repatriating its inhabitants' online data; other governments in the region soon joined the choir. Further centralization of this data led to the creation of a strategic genetic reserve for each country's citizenry.

In Argentina, every individual was obliged to have a national ID card thanks to a law promulgated under one of the military dictatorships. Beginning with the first infant born in 2012, the government gathered biometric information including fingerprints and digitalized face scans from all newborns in a Ministry of Genetics database that quickly grew to encompass millions of individuals. Data from network technologies involving cellular phones, credit cards, and public transportation usage were later added, creating "life trajectories" warehoused at both the center and the headquarters of the ministry. By this point, the Regional Reorganization Plan had been adopted throughout Latin America, creating immense repositories of "persons in a state of trajectory"—that is, alive. Then the exhumations began, yielding collections of brains that offered a genetic context for the demographic past. In order to analyze this massive flood of information, however, a number of technological leaps were still required, and this is where Max Lambard and the Stromatoliton team came into the picture.

The Patagonian tech hub centered on the Balseiro Institute had come into being thanks to the digital arms race and the laxity of local laws. The enthusiasm with which the governments of Brazil and Argentina signed agreements on shared biometric analysis was held up as a demonstration of the region's geopolitical strength. While the DNA reproduction centers in Iquitos played a decisive role in establishing the overall configuration of power, the Balseiro Institute worked more closely with the duty-free bioelectronic development zone in Manaus, which was dedicated to the massive incubation of data analysis companies; one of the largest DNA databases off of which Stromatoliton fed was located there. And as was confirmed from political pulpits throughout the continent, the defense of regional DNA databases was the final bastion of nation-state power in the twenty-first century.

Piera wondered how Max had first been drawn to the Project. She imagined him calculating his approach, emotionless, tuned with the parameters of his ambition. In his early press conferences, he referred to the importance of redefining history in terms of experiments; he emphasized that he'd first been attracted to the Project's experimental components, and their potential for innovation.

Untainted by the concerns of the establishment, he had dedicated himself to building out his dream. He passed through all the key universities, dropping out shortly; he studied in the department of exact sciences in Buenos Aires just long enough to meet Riccardo, with whom he would form a trailblazing company in the particularly complex new field of IT security. A polyglot in terms of scientific notation, his ability to understand what was being said to him in various languages allowed him to establish immediate bonds of trust with other brilliant young minds, and occasionally he could provide the overarching vision they lacked. At the moment we met him, his destiny was asserting itself through the elite technocratic lobbying he undertook to influence the decisions of the G-22.

Lambard foresaw that, given the exponential adoption pattern of sequencing and processing technology, information permitting a company to locate individuals in genetic-temporal space, to geolocalize the specificity of their persons, to re-create their vital trajectories on the world's newly unfolded map, would be of incalculable value. Up until the year 2015, social networks found themselves merely *in possession* of the elements of which each individual is constituted, as defined by the reductive parameters of their social and familial relationships, their interests and preferences and consumption patterns, their education and secret Web searches. This enormous amount of data represented a new world to be discovered, but the senses—the touch, the vision—required to make sense of its labyrinthine nature did not yet exist. A Leviathan built of techniques for apprehending and interpreting the data would have to be assembled, but the computing power necessary to calculate individual trajectories, to identify individual signals amidst the noise of all others, was still out of reach. Max Lambard's quantum leap consisted precisely of betting on the low-cost creation of technology that didn't yet exist but would soon result in cheap quantum computers with specific functions. This ambitious move allowed him to generate a wave of prestige that guaranteed him eventual access to the data; it was also strategically brilliant, as it paved the way for him to monetize the construction of his parallel project, the one that really mattered to him: Stromatoliton.

He'd borrowed his idea for Stromatoliton from one of the oldest living structures on Earth. Stromatolites—literally, "stone carpets"—are dynamic structures that expand through the stratification of particules effected primarily by cyano-bacteria. Some of these small stone-like formations are more than a billion years old, and they can be found throughout the most inhospitable deserts on the planet—a fossilized inva-sion of terrestrial coral reefs, an extremophile culture of small round cacti made of stone. According to Max, the structure of human history closely resembles that of stromatolites: a multitudinous colony's petrified characteristics, with some residual action on the surface; a vitreous foam made of the past, codified by a given species; a living expansion deter-mined, in practice, by calcified foundations built of their own excrement. It wasn't a romantic vision, or a prophetic one. He limited himself to considering human actions as physical elements, a category of things within an alternate space with its own temporal rules and chemical laws.

The regional DNA databases made the public at large party to the silent revolution under way. Once available for analysis, the data showed genetic trajectories, a living public portrait of the concrete but typically opaque lives of individuals. Each trajectory functioned as an informational stand-in that could be consulted without involving its *conscious* human vector—as a political substitute that wouldn't interfere with naked life but that reflected it in all its quantifiable aspects.

Piera was aware of Max's reputation, and knew that there had to be a B side to this history, but until now she hadn't seen any traces of it. For the moment, her own personal interest in an up-close look at the sensorial apparatus producing such unbridled biometrics was sufficient. For her, it was only in crevices like this that science found a propitious growth medium for reproducing and advancing. She didn't know why she felt so strongly that she had to be present for something so openly sinister; perhaps her need to see it in person was just the result of her own morbid scientific curiosity. (When she'd notified her manager, Jeremy, that she was quitting to go back to Argentina, his mind had filled with horses on wide plains—the typical Texan fantasy of a healthy, sinful life of massive cuts of beef and moral laxity. "Patagownia! Awesome. I envy you, and not so secretly.")

As for the atomic center: as Leni Waskam soon informed her, its past tied straight into the nation's own. Ronald Richter—a disciple of Heisenberg in Germany, and one of Kurt Tank's cronies—had successfully mutated from citizen of the Third Reich to inhabitant of Rio Negro. He built a secret laboratory on Huemul Island, a rocky promontory of bushes and steppes in the middle of Nahuel Huapi, with the objective of harnessing the energy of atomic fusion to build a hydrogen bomb—a project the Germans hadn't managed to finish before the Americans ended the war. The decision to build the lab was the result of a synaptic quantum leap on the part of General Perón, who had trained as a soldier in Mussolini's Italy, was an age-old ally of the Axis powers, and wanted to join the market of global nuclear powers.

Magnificently enriched during the European wars, the Argentine leadership had at its disposal an army of machines, materials, and specialized personnel to support Richter's odyssey. He pursued his research amidst absolute secrecy, as befitted a supreme technology of war. He surrounded the island with security agents he knew personally, ordering them not to allow anyone to approach the island.

Alarmed by the excessive secrecy and the expenses involved, a physicist was sent out to investigate. The report that José Antonio Balseiro turned in was a death sentence for the Project; he testified to the fact that there was no evidence of successful atomic fusion. Richter's star fell, together with that of Perón, and the new military government banished the previous regime. Peronism was now thought of as a malignant hallucination, and Richter had fed that hallucination with the help of the public purse. Faced with ensuing chaos, a group of Argentine physicists led by Balseiro decided to make use of the personnel and technological structures already in place. Locating the atomic center in Patagonia would provide it with a healthy autonomy from the public universities, which were subject to the typical ups and downs of local power. Bariloche thus played a vital peripheral role in the fundamental madness of the twentieth century; that the Argentine technological village had been founded by a Nazi made its reality all the more palpable. In fact, having a Nazi involved in the birth of the Project's program to analyze the genetic content of Latin America's inhabitants wasn't a historical irony—it was, rather, a perfect inevitability, according to Ema Cattelan, the center's new director.

The Stromatoliton group was a novelty within the Balseiro Institute. Understood as a new phase of Max Lambard's megalomania, it had captured the attention of the flamboyant Cattelan. Tall, attractive, much younger than the *senatus* members who made up most of the board, she had been given a hand up by César Rábida, who saw her as a competent administrator whose ambitions—necessarily bracketed, he thought, by the fact of her young family—would make her an ideal proxy, a perfect means for keeping his own power intact.

After three decades of professional obsession, César wanted, for the first time in his life, to be a bourgeois scientist: one with ample free time to indulge his Patagonian hobbies of seven-hour lamb roasts and sailing excursions across the frigid waters of Nahuel Huapi. He wasn't willing to abandon the monarchical/granular style with which he had run the center, but he was sure that Ema would let him take the wheel for important decisions. There was a tacit pact within the golden circle of senior leadership: they would maintain control *until the bitter end*, an end that the center's measured entry into "new maturity" wasn't meant to hasten. They had seen the country rise from its own ashes several times, and had accumulated all the knowledge produced by a pair of scientific revolutions, the nuclear and the computational. For César, the country's scientific course never stopped being a personal matter. His peak was accompanied, however, by a few surprises: the golden circle was spinning down some unexpected paths.

Long gone were the days of L'Electrón Fou, the nightclub inside the atomic center where students and eminent scientists danced spastic Twists in the craziest nights that Bariloche could remember; long gone was the secret uranium enrichment project begun in the late 1970s during the Dictatorship. Now that they averaged sixty years of age, the pastimes of the leading engineer team were the same ones they had as teenagers. Pacho and Raúl, members of the golden circle leading the center's most intimate maneuvers, had both become enamored of backstreet drag racing. They went out at night to race on Avenida Bustillo or the road to the airport, covered by dark; even now, the road to the local airport had never installed public lighting. They gathered in their mansions, away from their wives, and staged competitions between malbecs and cabernets from Cuyo and Cafayate. They reminisced about their epic rise from physics students to unequaled scientists; their lives unfolded more pleasurably in a state of nostalgia. And once the men were again half-unconscious with drink, a friendly driver took the guests to their respective homes.

Shortly after she was named to the post, Ema Cattelan dedicated herself to reorganizing the center. A summer thick with board-member vacations gave her the opportunity to create distinguished new titles for the members of senior management who "had reached the height of their uselessness," as she commented at an informal breakfast with Max. (She'd learned the phrase from César.) With the help of Sofía Ronell, César's former secretary, Ema matched the starting date of each new post to the end of the relevant board member's time off. The two women took pleasure in striding together up the hallways of the center: Sofía, a perfumed being with high heels and net stockings that were destabilizing in the rural/scientific context of the center; and Ema, dressed more modestly, little given to displays of any sort, wearing ultralight mountaineering sunglasses that made her all the more mysterious.

Preferring terse elegance to ostentation, Ema separated the engineering brontosauri from all real areas of corportate influence. (Suddenly, the center was being referred to as "the company.") She thought it important to diversify their research, and encouraged the rapid development of patents on which new tech firms could be based. Quickly and silently, she expanded the budget and invested in start-ups all over the Southern Cone, creating alliances with the tech hubs in Manaus and Iquitos, facilitating agreements that leap-frogged the center's bureaucracy on their way down the corridor of BRIC banking initiatives.

The atomic center was now partnering with companies it had helped to create. The new model infuriated the board, because it had been developed behind their backs, and even more because of its simplicity and efficiency. Perceived as unfamiliar with the workings of the machine, the two women had created a blueprint for its reform; from the point of view of César, who'd been "promoted" to *senatus*, it was clearly the work of two Yoko Onos undermining the center's legacy.

It took Piera a week to tour all of the center's intricately entwined units and laboratories. At last she was taken underground to see the clean room, where most of the genetic material was stored. The quantum heart of Stromatoliton was found on the next floor down, accessed by a dedicated staircase that was separate from the workaday maze of hallways and pass codes.

The first time that Piera saw Cassio standing upright, he was coming out of the elevator, his backpack like a hump high on his back. He looked like a six-year-old boy with a rare case of acromegaly, floating against the wind in a heavy jacket. At the moment they were walking side by side, their hands in their pockets.

In the debriefing videos, Cassio had noticed that Piera looked a bit like Snow White, lover of dwarves; his inner dwarf now noted a slight resemblance to Monica Lewinsky as well. Monica had disconcerted him as a child. He remembered her interrogation with independent counsel Kenneth Starr, and her declaration: "I want to make it clear that I was the first one to have an orgasm." Cassio pushed the image away—he didn't want to become aroused.

Piera stopped at one of the windows that gave onto a white laboratory. Her mouth went back and forth between a smile and something else.

"You were here in the beginning, right?"

Piera kept her Monican eyes on him. That the mythic intern should have saved the dress stained with her lover's semen—that she manually preserved the DNA—that's what made her a visionary. Finally part of Cassio's brain was activated for speech:

"The theoretical foundation required to build Stromatoliton was already in place back in 2011. And the computational power that we needed already existed in nature—it's straight physics. But we didn't have the ability to channel it, and we didn't have the data. Are you plugged in?"

Piera shook her head.

Cassio had read that the story (the crime) began when Monica lifted her short skirt to surreptitiously show her thong as she left the Oval Office. An infantile gesture, irresponsible, so twentieth century, when human behavior was controlled by nothing but mental machinery. He blinked several times before deciding to continue:

"Okay, so then you're not emitting anything at the moment, but everyone who's plugged in is constantly transmitting personal data, and at the same time, each person becomes an informant on everyone else, because their position in the web gives away the positions of everyone in their node— when an individual data stream dries up, the node informs on whoever is missing. All the information captured by the sensors of everyone who's plugged in is sent to the Ministry of Genetics. Thanks to the deal that Max set up, from there it's sent to Stromatoliton, where for the first time ever we have the capacity to process it."

(Piera was amused by the fact that when confronted with the task of describing technology to neophytes, beings like Cassio always adopted a phony didactic approach. She herself wasn't immune to the tendency. A few days before, while walking through downtown Bariloche in search of a vegetarian restaurant with a small group of programmers, she had caught herself pointing out Bionoses haloed in pink light beneath the security cameras mounted on most of the light posts and traffic lights they passed. She'd learned a great deal while working on the Bionose project, and was particularly proud of what they'd accomplished. As one of the top thirty or so employees of the global Bionose team, she had worked at the local office of the UN's Biological Weapons Monitoring Commission. The noses were installed in every city in the world; they sniffed the air in search of tiny fragments of DNA, sequenced them in real time, and sent them to a centralized data bank. There they were compared to known pathogenic agents, and simulations were run to determine their interactions within a variety of generic systems. The growing ease with which DNA could be sequenced had put the ability to produce and distribute lethal viruses within reach for absolutely anyone, at least in theory. Well aware of the threat of tsunami-like epidemics, WHO was leading the drive to develop a shield: an artificial immunological system covering the surface of the Earth. For the moment it was only creating a genetic map of the world, but the next step would be to equip the noses themselves with DNA sequencers and counteragents capable of inoculating the local population immediately against known threats. Cassio had been observing her openly while she talked: the hiking boots, the thermal underwear, the fluorescent North Face jacket with its hood, the fading blue strands of hair across her forehead. He'd had several questions, but didn't ask them; instead he'd nodded in the direction of Covita, the vegetarian restaurant on Bustillo. The owner, one of the Institute's prodigal daughters, said hello with a faint bow of her head.

Cassio and Piera turned up the hallway, walking side by side. Two men in white lab coats were walking toward them. They said hello, but stiffly—a collateral effect of Piera's presence. Cassio waited for them to disappear around a corner before continuing:

"When the grid is complete, we'll have the ability to cross-reference each person's trajectory with the traces collected by the specific cameras and noses located at every business, in every public facility, on every road that falls along that individual's space-time line. Of course, calculating even a single trajectory used to take huge amounts of time and an unheard-of processing capacity. But with Stromatoliton, we have the ability to trace the trajectories of entire populations all at once. Millions of people. We always knew that taken together, genetic background and consumption patterns and space-time lines would offer an objective history of each individual, but the data wasn't readable by any machine. That is, the algorithms could read the lives, but we couldn't read the algorithms. The data was there, like in the genome, but we still had to sharpen the tools that could make it legible."

Cassio could barely contain his enthusiasm.

"And now we can. It's as if we've created an invisible and incredibly powerful animal that is ours to train."

The animal of the state unleashed, thought Piera.

"And are you plugged in?" she asked.

"No. I belong to the other side. Like you."

Piera looked in through the windows at the immaculate containers that held the mysterious genetic deposits. Then she turned back to him. His face was different, as if the room in the light had dimmed.

"But everybody already knows all this," she said.

Cassio was calmly startled, but the situation itself didn't make him uncomfortable; he liked having her eyes on him. He concentrated on not blinking. And now Piera softly squeezed out the words:

"I think you brought me here to tell me something else."

This disconcerted him. The blue T-shirt visible beneath his lab coat neither rose nor fell. Piera waited to see if he'd say something that wasn't in the script.

He knew that there were others watching, infesting the white hallway walls; once discovered, they disappeared into the labyrinth. The two of them were now alone. How could a few dozen kilos of protein, fat, bone, and feathers be so sure of herself, so out of the ordinary, instead of simply *being*, like most things? Monica. Cassio stared at her, his hand flat against the glass.

"When we finished building Q-Co, the quantum computer, and began processing the data that we received, nothing made any sense. We couldn't draw any constellation of facts against the background noise. The data was intermixed, and the universe of possibilities was gigantic; for the first time ever we could explore it in its entirety, but no single story emerged as more probable than any other."

Piera pushed her hair back, listening carefully.

"It took us a while to realize that we didn't have the criteria to establish the proper limiting conditions. Now we know what we have to do to take advantage of the data—to make it, shall we say, an informant."

He looked at her Monican eyes, saw that he was there too, cuddled in the reflection of her glasses like a goldfish in a white romper.

"Can I see it?" she asked.

Cassio guided her to the end of the hallway. He opened a door, and they heard the peculiar hiss of air escaping from a pressurized room. The clean room was equipped with a series of filters to prevent contamination, and its air pressure and temperature were kept within established parameters.

Piera found herself standing before a seemingly infinite repository of living tissue. Small test tubes, each with computer-controlled valves, filled row after row of storage freezers; the tubes were petri dishes, their contents codified according to biological engineering protocols that every student was obliged to repeat over and over ad nauseam until they'd learned them by heart. It was clear at a glance that the underground freezers were full of traces of DNA; the codes on the labels confirmed that it was all human DNA. To judge by the number of test tubes per freezer, the number of freezers per row, and the number of rows, she was looking at the genetic material of no fewer than two hundred thousand people.

Cassio directed her back out into the hallway and closed the clean room door. He looked at her attentively, waiting. Then he spoke slowly:

"As we searched for the right limiting conditions to filter out the noise, we started feeding the machine with sequences of DNA taken from the exhumed cadavers of just a few individuals, picked more or less at random. And then everything began to make sense—the process really started to work. Certain parts of the story became clear, well-defined, and we understood that this was the path that would lead to a functional Stromatoliton. We don't know exactly why it works, or if it's going to work at scale. But Max made a deal with Bionose to start sucking in data from all over the country; the idea is that we'll turn that cloud of information into the densest possible definition of inhabited territory."

Piera thought for a few seconds. At first she spoke toward his hands, then raised her eyes.

"The thing is that with each human DNA sample, you're also taking in DNA from all of the other organisms of which the donor consists. The dust mites on the skin. Intestinal flora, phages, bacterial growths in the mouth . . . The human genome represents only ten percent of the cells that occupy our body space; the other ninety percent comes from the genomes of fungi, bacteria, protozoa. Like they say, percentage-wise, 'I' is mostly 'them.' And that's without even counting the epigenetic characteristics that influence the expression of different proteins. A plant—a flower, for example—will develop different modes according to its environment and the genetic content of its soil. Sun, rain, the minerals in the ground, but also the fungi, microbes, and insects that live alongside its roots and develop relationships with the plant. It's the same with humans. Which explains the results you're getting;

you're taking expanded samples from what is assumed to be a human history, but you're misreading the bacterial elements, and the samples are then subject to a temporal sequence—"

A voice interrupts:

"Hey. What are you guys doing?"

Leni Waskam is coming up the hallway. Piera and Cassio don't react right away.

"I don't have a freezer in my house, so I keep my food here in Tupperware. You want some? It's couscous with meatballs."

Cassio stares at him intently, hoping that Leni will suddenly become infected with some recently revived strain of smallpox. Leni smiles and chews with the air of a friendly alien.

"Not for me," says Piera. "I've got work to finish, but thanks."

She turns back to Cassio, her eyes bulging slightly.

"Let's continue this some other time, okay?"

"Should I go with you?"

"No thanks, I know how to get there."

They watched her go, her white lab coat dissolving in the light cast by the fluorescent tubes. For a few more seconds, Cassio stayed frozen in place. Leni ate very slowly, chewing his infinitesimal slices.

A few hours later, Cassio and Leni rebooted their friendship at the house of some friends of Leni's—Noelia and Ailín. *They are the resistance*, he'd murmured as he introduced them to Cassio. Ailín had dark hair, thin lips, a multicolor wool vest. Both she and Noelia painted their faces with black and white lines, disfiguring their features so they could go outside without being recognized by the ubiquitous cameras.

"The people of Bariloche are *asleep*," said Noelia. "Totally. Don't you realize that?"

Mossad, the black cat of the house, lifted an inquiring gaze.

Cassio had heard the same story over lunch: the previous day, the authorities had discovered the rat-eaten body of a climber who'd gotten lost on his way down from Laguna Negra. The rats had caught him alone. His face was still recognizable, but they had burrowed into his body with unusual voracity and thoroughness. He'd died of internal bleeding.

This type of event always incited Noelia to return to her obsession with moral decadence: the Earth was tired of our presence, and had certain strategies for dealing with us. The rats were one of those strategies. Didn't we see that all these calamities, all these crises, held messages for us?

"Guys, I can't explain the messages to you. Either you see them or you don't. They don't show themselves to just anyone."

Bovine and tranquil, Leni listened, pretending to be precisely the incisive, timid, visionary observer that he wasn't. Noelia went to the kitchen, brought back mugs of tea. She raised her mug toward Cassio, who returned the gesture. She invited them to try the gluten-free, salt-free food; she recycled everything, and you could smell the compost pile from the living room. Now she was telling Leni about the UFO she'd seen the previous night.

"You truly do have to keep your mind and heart open. Because the aliens are tired. Tired of *us*."

She offered him a bowl of garbanzo paste. Mossad swung his weight over against Cassio, who caressed him compassionately; Leni and Noelia exchanged glances and grimaces. Ailín looked at Cassio, smiled, blinked several times. Completely at ease, as if his pristine intentions had finally yielded some respect, Leni decided he was ready to assume a more masculine role: he offered to make more chai, and to bring in wood for a fire. The firewood proposal caused streamers of good humor in Noelia, though his plan had a serious flaw—the fireplace formed part of Mossad's feng shui circuit, the series of mysterious urinary mandalas with which he fought against alterity.

Noelia's mode of conversation dug its own tunnels without ever slowing down. Suddenly, it dove into her past as a puppeteer, back when she was studying arts and letters in the capital; moody Mossad had already become her companion.

"Were you in Buenos Aires in 2015?" she asked Cassio.

"Yeah, I think so."

"Where did you live?"

"Caballito."

"Near Puán?"

"Not too close. Where the J line comes through."

Her face lit up.

"So you must have seen it!"

"Seen what?"

"We're the ones who did it."

Leni interrupted:

"Noelia was part of the group that burned all those cars."

". . ."

"La Paternal, Caballito . . . You didn't read about it?"

Noelia seemed disappointed. Ailín stared at them, looking a bit like a rabbit.

"No, I never heard anything about it," said Cassio, fondly remembering his moped. "I guess I just didn't notice—maybe because I didn't have a car, or any emotional attachment to cars."

Noelia couldn't hold herself back any longer, stretched out her arms and recited:

"*A public, visible attack: burning cars as an offering to the ecosystem. You burn, but will you spurn? Will you spurn if you burn? Burn once and you'll yearn to burn! Alienated car owners, people the streets with your armed potential. Survive the catastrophe! Salvation through outrage, armor, and abandonment. We're betting on the madness of both flames and flamettes. Fear is the only thing that doesn't burn. We are our own fury, the fury of the universe set alight: we are the motor of the astral plane!*"

Mossad snuggled right up against Cassio and gave a soft, lost mew. Leni, on the other hand, still felt completely at ease. Sprawled out in the cane armchair, he winked at Noelia emphatically, but she was stirring pollen into her tea and didn't notice. He waited patiently as the fire monologue dissolved into a short elegy to water, which became a description of the Lagos del Sur aquifer, where the women would soon be headed—the location of earthly salvation. He was sure that this discourse on the humidity of things would end in some nondescript anarcho-ecologist cul-de-sac—the logos of nature, the reproductive cycle, the body as the giver of life and light. Then, perhaps, the metaphors would be replaced by what they represented; Noelia would take off her clothes and Leni would close his eyes and lick her body uninterruptedly until the time came to insert himself. He lifted his mug:

"To anarchist prose-poetry!"

Cassio looked down at where Ailín's concave organs lurked silently beneath her thick clothes. Just then there was a murmur, a damp clacking sound, air passing like a spirit from one end of her body to the other. Her heartbeat, his, those of Leni and Noelia as well; spoons trembling on the table, hands fanning like the wings of butterflies.

So this was the resistance. Noelia's speech hadn't impressed him. These women were just hippie luddites, and there was nothing particularly specific about their hatred. He wanted to ask Leni if the women knew what he and Leni did for a living, wanted to know to what degree they considered the men their enemies. How much information about the center's activities had filtered through to the outside world? It seemed absurd to him, the women's belief that by obscuring their features with paint they became invisible to the state; there were so many means of obtaining data now that facial recognition was practically trivial. The only way to hide was to become another species, to transform oneself into something else.

Mossad squinted as music came on—a Luis Alberto Spinetta song from 1988.

Everything lasts an instant,
It's better to be the wind,
Everything lasts an instant
All life long.

Ailín laid her head to rest next to the computer. Suddenly, Ailín and Noelia and Leni ceased to exist, and Cassio took up his lambskin jacket and petted Mossad, who meowed like a hoarse mockingbird. Cassio waved a liminal goodbye and was jettisoned out of the house. Violet glimmerings descended from the peak of the sky, covering everything, sliding down the side of the frozen mountain. Suddenly, his own trajectory painted itself sharply against the world.

He crossed the valley floor and headed downhill through an expanse of low trees and creeping vines. The tips of the mountain crags were lost in the clouds, and branches scraped at his ankles like tenterhooks. He could feel the animals around him, could almost hear their faint howls, could almost see their dead eyes.

A greenish glow seemed to filter up through the mist-filled underbrush; somewhere farther down, the lake oozed around the twisted roots of the trees. He heard the cries of bats muffled by the foliage. Overhead, branches drew themselves black against the sky like coral reaching up through the night at the bottom of the sea.

He entered an area dense with weeping bamboo. The stalks bristled up out of the earth in tall thickets, and the flowering had begun: every twenty-five years, *Chusquea culeou* goes into bloom, and many species of rats are drawn irresistibly to the blossoms, which contain a powerful rodentine aphrodisiac. The ensuing demographic explosions are known as rat storms. He passed through a tunnel formed of bowed stalks; he hoped their shape wasn't caused by the sheer weight of rats hiding in their crowns. He knew that they were everywhere around him, but none could be seen.

He was over forty now, but whenever he returned to the mountains he felt like one of Tolkien's hobbits still waiting to be assigned a mission. Life in Bariloche was peaceful enough; a model scientist, his daily focus was on the center and its life. Technical challenges were always the order of the day, and he could hardly complain of boredom, as his cortex was properly stimulated by his work on Stromatoliton. He heard a nearby squeak, felt others that were ghostly silent; at the end of the tunnel, the countryside opened up.

There were lights along the curved stone stairway that led to the top of a promontory where a small cabin rested on a foundation of stone and pilings. Outside there was a terrace full of dilapidated lounge chairs; inside was an old heating stove topped with ceramic tile, a small kitchen, scattered furniture. Something shone from the kitchen sink; the lights had been left low. Hovering over the banister was a face painted with pairs of asymmetrical triangles in black and white—like a singer for Kiss, but with stalagmites. Cassio frowned and walked closer. The face belonged to Max, who gave him a hug.

"You got here just in time. We've already handed out the bitcodes."

"And this?" said Cassio, gesturing at the triangles on Max's face.

"Monica Lewinsky did it for me—you like?"

"She's here?" murmured Cassio.

Max didn't seem to have heard, was busy hooking the new bitcodes that Leni and the others had brought. When he was done, they all smoked and watched as the creatures emerged from their hiding places. The whole process took almost an hour. At first it was just bursts of light from their eyes; then that light began to illuminate the shapes of the rest. They came down from the hills, a chaotic horde drawn to the tallow; they took the bitcode bait, and the solution entered their organism. One by one, the rats lost their sense of direction and began to glow a greenish blue. In the dark grass, they looked like constellations drawing and undrawing themselves beneath the meridian. As the substance made its way through their intestinal canals, their squeaking went hoarse; then the human ear became attuned, and the noise lost its demonic ratlike air, began to sound more like crickets.

Down below the house there were now tumults of rats; in some cases the glow extended down the spine all the way to the tail. After their initial euphoria, the rats became lethargic; this is when clear patterns began to emerge. Over on the human side, music was turned on—the intersexual crooning of Asaf Avidan, the psychedelic turns of the riverine band Los Síquicos Litoraleños—and some of Max's private harvest was rolled. This was their entertainment during the flowering of the weeping bamboo. There was no trace of Piera.

They puffed in silence, lying back on the lounge chairs, looking up at the motionless stars and down at the rats' trajectories.

"So you met the resistance," said Max, holding in the smoke.

Out of the corner of his eye, Cassio saw the lit joint suspended millimeters away from his face.

"Resistance?" he said, inhaling.

"Leni told me. He keeps an eye on them."

"We went to see some girls . . . and they had some shit painted on their faces just like you. You're not going to tell me that's what you—"

"Look! Orion!"

In the distance, the shining rat points were held for a moment in a static sketch of the constellation, then dissolved into the black. Max exhaled, fascinated.

Splayed out on his lounge chair, Cassio began to feel impatient. He wasn't particularly worried about the mass slaughter of the rats; after all, it was completely legal, considered a service to the community. It was Max—his face blurred by the low light and the paint, his attitude toward sectors of the world he didn't understand—that made Cassio anxious. He almost believed that Max was plotting something . . . because he obviously was plotting something, because enjoying the appearance of peace in the bosom of the state was hardly his thing. Together, Stromatoliton and the rat plague created a sort of emotional balance within the context of the Project, a plateau of triumph that didn't fit with what Cassio knew, or thought he knew, about Max. Had Max changed forever? Had he resigned as a commander of chaos in order to become just one more of capital's foot soldiers? And maybe Cassio, too?

They were quiet for a few minutes. At the far end of the terrace, the others were taking pictures with a star tracker, an instrument designed to follow the orbs through outer space. Instead they were tracing the maps drawn by the rats as they died.

"Day by day we know more and more about things, get better and better at manipulating them," said Max, as if continuing a conversation that had no end. "And day by day they get stranger. They pull away . . ."

He made a vague gesture toward the valley crisscrossed with green rays.

"You reach the outer limit of your neuronal city, and then you're nowhere. God doesn't know what we're building, because we're its creators, not him. Code is pure humanity, not some participant in the Platonic reality of mathematics. God has no idea what we're up to."

He threw an acorn into the distance.

"We have to understand these things as dark constellations—that's what the Incas called them. They organized the sky in terms of the dark regions between stars, the interior shapes with bright parameters. But what creates space for meaning isn't the bright dots or the presence of light—for dark constellations, the light is the noise. What matters is the darkness. And day by day we know more, we have more information, but from our position way down deep inside our dark constellation, we've lost view of the outline."

Cassio watched him take a slow, deep toke.

"We live in an era so demon-possessed that all we can do is practice goodness and justice from a position of deep clandestinity," Max murmured. "We've gone so far into the darkness that there's no separating it from us. There aren't any visible lights. Clandestinity is the only system left."

Cassio hurled down Pioneros Avenue at top speed. His 2016 Clio rose and fell, drawing the curves of the terrain. Alongside the road, the vegetation was thick with bushes and tall conifers that extended their extremities toward him. A shadow passed him. He slowed down.

Two silhouettes slid toward him, ghosts floating up the dark road. They were monstrous there outside his capsule, appeared to be gesturing, as if they wanted to say something to him. He slowed down some more. Now his headlights illuminated two long-boarders walking along the highway, only a few meters away as they skimmed past, dancers on a floor of black ice.

Which is when he saw it: an enormous lenticular cloud, its limpid pink standing out against the sky. Swan-like, bright white edges, soft overlapping scales, stretching out above the peak of Cerro López, rising slowly. In his entire life he'd only seen a handful of these clouds, all of them high in the mountains, 3,500 meters or more, when he'd gone up to spend the night. Its appearance here seemed meteorologically impossible, on the order of cosmic magic. Cassio blinked.

Maybe he wasn't thinking clearly. Maybe he'd spent his cerebral life focused on whatever happened to catch his attention rather than on what defined the landscape. *What matters is the internal face of the nebula, the dark constellation. We are the ones who decide which things are stars.*

His profession was based on the world's legibility; its blank zones were what made it accessible to humans. Darkness made legible became luminous. Soon there would be nowhere to hide. Ontological caves would cease to exist. Only the stellar trajectories would sustain the contrast, the one and the zero, light and darkness. At any given moment, all over the world there were bots awakening. They flickered, stretched out, launched their golemic selves, joined the swarming multitude.

He turned off his headlights, followed the lenticular cloud as if he were the one rising into the heights, as if what came undone in the sky would soon spread everywhere else. He would become the noise inside the virus, the meat that would make it both real and completely random; his mind had run the numbers. The arteries that channeled the blood now formed part of a more complex system of concavities. He felt the vertigo of self-discovery, tried to bury himself once again in the formless mass of the rest of reality—in everything that wasn't *him*. But he too was real. He would be the portal between two worlds. *Are you going to kneel before the darkness, or are you going to fight?* The shapes formed by known stars howled in the black abyss above him. The Clio pushed on, mimicking the night.

He walked up the glass-lined corridor and turned on the light. It was four A.M. or so. Onto a spiral staircase that burrowed straight down to the coldest part of the building, where the heart of Q-Co was kept just a few degrees Kelvin above absolute zero. Next to Q-Co was the mother lab: repository of living tissue, traces of DNA from thousands of people, the initial samples.

Walking again, through a door, and now he saw that the far end of the hallway was lit up. No one was supposed to be here at this hour. He made his way slowly down the hall, alert to the slightest change in the light.

"Monica?"

He realized that he'd said it out loud. He had called to her, like in his dreams, and here she was, composed entirely of herself: Piera. She looked at him with half a smile. Cassio stopped beside the window that gave onto the room holding the machine. A ray of light from a more distant machine swept across his face.

"I need your help."

n the course of the day, they hardly even exchange glances. After lunch, Piera goes to the year-end speech that Ema Cattelan gives beside Newton's apple tree, a sapling planted in the library garden, descendant of the original. The speech is met with applause and some quiet coughs; the day is full of dust, a Calima-like yellowish haze embracing the earth. Piera sheaths her face with a scarf, spies on the world through the slit she's left for her eyes. She's nervous, and excited to see what perspective the night will bring. When she returns to the laboratory, she doesn't see Cassio anywhere.

Cassio awoke with a jolt. He'd been dreaming of spiders lowering toward him, crawling slowly across his lips.

The circular light above him was so powerful it hurt his eyes. He squeezed them shut; when he tried to move his hand he realized that he was wired up. Now Piera's head eclipsed the lamp, and she smiled at him through the exorbitant light. She showed him the stinger in her hands: a syringe half-full of precious cargo. Cassio shuddered in light terror, realized he'd done so when Piera laughed and caressed his head.

"We can abort the mission whenever we want—don't forget that."

Cassio shook his head and relaxed there on the bed, remembering their conversation.

So it could be said that this machine is the place where computer viruses and biological viruses live together in the same medium— the same ecosystem.

It's still dark outside, but they have to get out of the subterranean lab before their colleagues start coming in, can't let themselves be found anywhere near it. Cassio suggests going to get breakfast somewhere with a view of Nahuel Huapi. Pleased with himself, with the strength of his convictions, he helps her put on her coat.

They walk along the big avenue beside the lake, past the cathedral designed by Bustillo in the 1940s, its immense *vitreaux* bearing images of natives assassinating clerics. To one side is a disco called Cerebro, blue and neon fuchsia. To the other, the silent mountains navigate the lunar stillness.

Up the street comes a group of adolescents still drunk from the night before—they can barely walk. Cassio watches Piera out of the corner of his eye.

"Have you been to Chile?" he asks.

"When I was a girl. Valparaiso. I don't remember it at all."

"Puerto Montt isn't far from here."

"I know, but I didn't go. I'd love to, though."

"It's right on the other side of these mountains."

"Yeah . . ."

"You really should go. They have this bivalve food festival."

"Do they?"

Piera looks at him, suddenly alert.

"Marine fauna is amazing," he says.

"Ribbed mussels[1] are good," she concedes.

Cassio stares at her intensely.

"And Chilean abalone,"[2] he says.

"And choro mussels,"[3] she answers immediately.

No one is going to beat her at Chilean mollusks.

"Pink clams,"[4] he says.

"King crab."[5]

1 Ribbed mussels   2 Chilean abalone   3 Choro mussels

4 Pink clams   5 King crab

"Mayonnaise."

"Not actually a seafood."

"But an essential element in the Chiloé Island diet."

They walk on silently. Swirls of incandescent beams advance above them like heavenly armies, wreathing the earth's southernmost atmosphere in pinkish tones that scatter as the light grows.

Beneath the surgical lamp, Cassio smiled. He opened his eyes, let the light burn his pupils a bit. Piera leaned in close, her lips parted. She was focused on expelling the air from the syringe, and it seemed to Cassio that her lips were even redder now, she was more Snow White, more Monica Lewinsky than ever, and yet completely herself. He was on the verge of leaving his anthropoidal specificity behind, melding himself astrally with the interior of the machine, and he tried to think of something to say, knowing that nothing but her voice would stay with him as he descended beyond the shoreline where his fellow humans grazed. A chill ran through his tennis-shoed feet. Had the fever started already? It wasn't supposed to begin for a few minutes more.

"I just have to get used to feeling feverish, right?"

She leaned over him and put a finger across his lips, opened her eyes wide and stared straight into his. Her lips at his ear:

"I haven't given you the shot yet."

A moment later a beam of light shot through his chest. Cassio exhaled; the drug made its way toward his extremities and began to do its work. He babbled for a time, then fell into a deep sleep.

The previous week had been grueling. They'd only finished

preparing the virus in Balseiro's DNA sequencer a few hours ago. This was Piera's first experiment involving a computer virus, and Cassio's first with a biological one; for the first time, in addition to being the demiurge, he would be the vector of contagion. As he lost consciousness, Piera listed these landmark achievements to herself—she would have to find some canned juice to celebrate. It occurred to her that they were now junkies addicted to a drug they'd only just invented. Not bad, not bad at all.

Cassio was still asleep; part of his face looked like it was immersed in a pond, with fluid circles moving about beneath his eyelids. The needle had done its work, sent the drug navigating silently through his waterways. For a few seconds he'd felt the skin of his face changing color: the veinlets shimmered yellow, then green around his red nostrils. It couldn't be seen, was only a sensation. Now he snorted, took a deep breath. His face gleamed as if in the light of a faint green halo.

He looked like a gigantic child there in the bed—or, better, like the carapace of a child enclosing an attractive man. Piera thought about smelling him while he slept, and the thought itself impressed her as the sort of thing that others would respect. She told herself that the impulse itself couldn't be helped given how nervous she was about the experiment—but she didn't want to unleash processes that she might not be able to control. It seemed ironic that her Victorian instincts would lead her to contemplate these details of fleshy desire right after she'd shot a virus into Cassio's veins. The monitors showed that his condition was stable. And he was cute like this, asleep—he looked like he could be trusted.

ven before I arrived, I knew that the ants here were bigger than the mammals. I knew that the evolutionary advances of certain local species shouldn't be compared to those in parts of the world restrained by the presence of gods and men. Here, nature displays its brutality plainly. With no god to emulate or religion to follow, they confront their mirror madly . . . I looked at them, tried to choke back my disdain, and thought, What kind of god would want to live among them?

The palace of Tartare d'Hunval was sunk in darkness. Something not entirely of this world had colonized his journal entries: *I feel that when I am writing, a dose of the fog takes me over.* And he wrote of a strange presence at the gathering the night before: a corpulent man whose face he never saw.

Who could have stolen the glass chest? *Absolutely anyone and everyone, but who?* Tartare wrote, clearly irritated. He'd made a list of all those who were present. Could it have been Guillaume de Barbosa, the first to describe *Stanhopea numinosa* on Brazilian soil? He was there without a doubt, though no one can remember what he was wearing. Perhaps Arielus Languis and Karl Stu made off with it? No one had seen either of them leave. Or maybe the emperor himself? Everyone knew about his fondness for magical instruments—his collection of photographs rivaled the biggest in Europe.

This morning Tartare had asked Zizinho not to touch

anything or clean up. He didn't yet have a name, but at least he and Niklas could do what they did best—they collected samples. They put everything they found in a wooden bookcase with glass doors:

A very fine silk handkerchief stained with crimson lipstick; two reddish hairs; an invitation on which the smell of a perfumed hand could still be detected; scraps of cloth; and dozens of goblets from which people had drunk. To this day the collection serves as a reconstruction of life in their milieu. And considered together with the list of guests, it is clear testimony to Tartare's interest in inner lives.

The following morning, still disfigured with rage at the loss of the glass chest, Tartare analyzed the samples with chemicals he had harvested. Meanwhile, who was that girl with the white skin and the worms? Both Niklas and Tartare had seen her in the course of their hallucinations: extremely pale, the worms adorning her arm, entering her veins below the humerus.

Then it was time for Tartare's snail bath. Zizinho had gathered them earlier in the day, and placed them patiently all over his master's tense visage. A few steps away, quite comfortable in his wooden armchair, Niklas ate an apple and read the journal of the local geographical institute. Most of the snails tried to find a way down off of Tartare's face; a few of them nested contentedly beside his nose, leaving behind circular steles of themselves. With his eyes closed and one snail sliding across his eyelid, Tartare's mouth never stopped moving. He proposed and then discarded several theories. He was certain that there had been nonhumans amongst his guests.

After lunch, the two men headed upriver. It was like returning to the moment of Creation, when vegetation surged up all over the planet. Niklas once again sensed the outlines of his own hallucination: the overgrown meadows, the taste of the swamp in his mouth. The meadows dissolved at the banks of iridescent streams, and trees stood out like castles, lowering their branches only to raise them again, lines of dense liquid vegetal matter uniting the earth and sky.

They pushed forward, and a cloud-like mist swathed the foliage; they could see nothing but a few trees that rose only to disappear like ghosts overhead, and a few rock pinnacles left behind as they descended toward the hidden crater. The law of mud reigned in all directions: wherever they looked they saw the swamp unfolding, a labyrinth of hidden hands, the forgotten hands of the enormous beings that shuddered beneath the river. Niklas closed his eyes to save the images, and his hand moved across the cover of his journal.

Everything speaks until we stop looking.

He noted the pink dolphins swimming alongside them; then for hours there was no other visible trace of animal life, only the towering trees rising up between the shadows and the clouds—terrifying. And suddenly they couldn't see anything at all. The last sight Niklas would remember is that of Tartare descending slowly, knee-deep in the water, his pant legs pulled up to his thighs.

They woke deep in the jungle. There was a musty smell, something like that of an abandoned library. They couldn't believe their eyes. A palace rose above the trees in a cone of shadow.

They entered through a wide hall that led to the crater, and followed a lit passage to a room carved out underground. It was a splendid palace, and at the same time it was a horror of decadence. At the edge of the crater there was a vast salon, the floor covered in ancient tiles of brittle stone where the roots of the trees and the pathways worn by rats now intertwined. There was a long wooden table that appeared not to have been used in centuries, and some silverware laid out for a banquet frozen in time. Blue ivy had found its way up and around massive chairs that looked like medieval thrones; the vines crossed through the air and united to form a dome above them. In the gaps between the vines, the sky opened out a shining white.

They heard sounds coming from a softly lit courtyard, and made their way toward it. A small lamp circulated its light slowly over slabs of mica set like stone mirrors in the walls. A cumulus cloud of insects gave form to a dark network of hammocks. *The laboratory.* There were men smoking and talking amongst themselves. They didn't seem to be paying any attention to the hammocks, where several naked women lay insensate.

Strange sounds were coming from a contiguous room—a velvet-covered ball of murmuring, and a few sonorous laughs. A thin voice could be heard imploring the others: *Enough, I'm begging you!* More laughter followed.

From back behind the hammocks there emerged a rotund and pale presence sheathed in a tuxedo and cape. *The corpulent eminence.* The mysterious collector who had visited Tartare's majestic cabinet room. *At first he looked to me to be six and a half feet tall; he had a glass of punch in his hand, and a captive audience.*

At times the man's voice lowered slowly until it almost disappeared, like the eyes of a crocodile easing beneath the surface of a swamp. Half-hidden in the darkness, he let his voice glide humidly past the women, chivalrously blinding his other guests. His words turned divinely in the air until the whole room was thick with mud; he asked aloud if there had ever been a profession more violent and sublime than that of hunting and capturing orchids.

Ever since the emperor decided to let zoologists, astronomers, ornithologists, and naturalists join the new imperial court, there's always been someone like this around.

Now Arielus Languis took the floor. He greeted Tartare and Niklas as if this was all merely a continuation of the gathering at Tartare's house. He acted completely naturally; his voice showed a certain enthusiasm, though he kept the volume low. Perhaps he didn't wish to waken the naked women who appeared

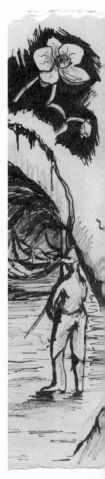

to be slumbering in the hammocks. He described his current research project to Tartare and Niklas, told them of places in the jungle that harbor snakes who enter the body through any given hole and respond to every stimulus. His slogan was, "They won't leave you any deader than you already are."

Arielus and Karl Stu denied having anything to do with the glass chest. They were working on a book that was, in their words, fundamental, as it would provide revolutionary new inroads for natural history. It was a sort of biography of the orchid genus *Mormodes*, describing a key moment in its creative mutation. They claimed that *Mormodes* served as a hinge between insect and plant: some generations lived as insects, others as flowers, and at times it retreated to its former life as a mushroom, jumping hundreds of generations back in time.

Tartare remained incredulous. According to information he'd received, these two men were less interested in documenting new species than in inventing them, in blending them together frenetically. *They head into the jungle looking for ways to create creatures with extra anuses. It's just another subterfuge, another way to fight off the darkness—every species does this.*

Nothing had prepared Niklas and Tartare for any part of this apparition. But they had heard tell of hordes of rats that wait until the world's light dims, then head out to hunt, crawling through tunnels, through weeds. Their eyes are red, and the skin on the palms of their feet is pink, practically human in appearance. At times the groups include humans who wear the skins of animals they've killed and use art beyond language to communicate, to organize the attacks.

But up to that point neither Niklas nor Tartare had ever witnessed any such thing.

As if reading their thoughts, the eminence spoke again. Tartare transcribes his words as follows:

I have become visible to you. Now leave behind the rainbow of pure venom, the black water.

He smiled. His cape lifted a few centimeters off the floor.

There are so many things that are watching us, things we can't see.

Niklas felt as though he were remembering thoughts he'd never had, thoughts that nonetheless formed part of him, as much a part as his very arm, or the hand that now held the bubbling glass of *salep.*

That was hundreds of moons ago. Refined men such as yourselves will have heard of the rats who took your species by surprise, who abandoned the lowlands and now roar their ferocious aria amidst the jungle symphony.

According to Niklas's journal, this is the moment at which he began to draw and describe everything that he saw. What he saw, however, appears to have had no clear form. It seems more as if he were sketching the thoughts that cover things—as if he were describing a velvet mantle instead of the object it protects and delineates.

There are species that don't evolve as such. They only grow in power. They spread themselves widely, like stains conquering a surface millimeter by millimeter—not for them the verticality of great depths or aerial conquest. And

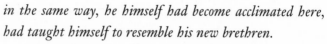

in the same way, he himself had become acclimated here, had taught himself to resemble his new brethren.

The eminence came a few steps closer. For the first time Niklas and Tartare could see his face clearly, though they couldn't believe what they were seeing. The man was a rat six feet tall, who said, in perfect and derisive human speech:

Most definitely, I did it for me and not for them . . . I never would have lowered myself to address such inferior beings face-to-face. I was a mint, the only mint that could create a certain golden coin, one that didn't yet exist in this world and yet bewitched it. During my first seasons among men, they found me startling; they feared me, but what they feared more was the sight of my potential made manifest. They had everything they needed to make themselves a deadly race; they dug deep into the ground, mastered the terrible beauties of the underworld, and yet were bewildered to find themselves the closest thing on Earth to a transparent primate . . . loyal to their own instincts, surely, but febrile without ever having known fever. Do you understand? I believe that you do, that I can detect in you some small certainties about me—I won't ask for proof, will be happy simply to believe you. I have spent my life among men procuring solace for my own species, and for the burning heat of the transformation for which I have come, a heat that creeps quickly along the fingers of those who seek darkness. Didn't you hear the words of the strangers? The words you too should have said? Darkness reigns in this region, which is why we organize the stars,

*coterminous on our maps—the true map is dark, and full of the
holes in our minds.*

*Sometimes I see them draw near . . . I can smell the blood that
they mistake for piety or knowledge. I feel them close to me, feel
the rumbling tumult of their rags and commerce, watch them
enter my lands . . . and then the black hole of the jungle swallows
them. What did I know of them? you will ask. I can only say that
wherever I went among them, the light of the moon had gone out.
What did they see with those elemental eyes? They saw nothing
before them but the mire, likewise elemental, and yet they sought
distance . . . distance from all that makes sense in these lands. In
their company, at times I thought of how fungi create themselves
precisely by dissolving themselves in other species . . . they take
what they can find, and disappear. The fact that on this side of
the human world, atrocities bear lizard wings and yet crawl
along the ground—this fact reveals something.*

His manners were indisputably refined, and as Arielus
never stopped pointing out, his collection of specimens was
unparalleled—it was in a completely different league from
those of Europe.

*At that moment he stretched out his arm, and I saw his gaunt
hands clearly, a sickly pink shade. He gestured toward the crater.
His horrible rat teeth shone as he spoke, sealing his pact with the
face of darkness under his command. I then thought that his life as
a rat was only an instrument, a way to show us, like an emissary
of light, the hidden evil, the death that stalks us, the shadows of
the human heart.*

The rat was a descendant of the Bragança y Pombal
dynasty. He had arrived on a ship from across the Atlantic,

a stowaway in first class escaping vassalage under Napoleon. He'd then made his way by river, hiding in dark crevices at first, managing to meddle his way into high society on the basis of pure charm. His talent for handling hallucinogenic substances opened the heavy gates; the spell he cast would not have been complete without his strange potions, which allowed him to traverse the mud-choked rivers as easily as the lavish halls that outline the lives of the local aristocracy in darkness.

We can't look directly at it. We must infer its shape, seeing in the dark the way one does when looking at the night sky.

The women of the aristocracy had never seen a being like this, and each kept the secret until all of them had enjoyed the novelty. The hallucinatory visions he gave them caused the women to forget about his appearance entirely. In a hundred years of appearing and disappearing, of sinking into the weeds and resurfacing amongst the humans of Rio, making and unmaking himself before their eyes, Hoichi had built an empire of darkness.

Everything can become something else. That is the teaching of the jungle, my friends. You see, nothing prevents me from being human, or from ceasing to be one whenever I please. Your name is . . .

"Tartare d'Hunval. And this is Niklas Bruun."

He took them to the small garden where he grew *Crissia pallida* inside the sleeping bodies. Tartare didn't dare ask about the glass chest. Niklas thought that among the sleeping women he recognized the girl he'd seen as he lay dreaming in Tartare's house. He closed his eyes, could almost feel her next to him.

The entire system of caves and goblets is designed to allow us to hide from the light; the jungle itself is such a system, permitting worms to bury their heads.

The rat exhaled the smoke from his cigarette little by little, and as it rose, it dissipated around his pink muzzle. This was his vision of humanity, the historiography of a group of worms spreading out across the landscape; he was the foreign species, but built his argument from a position of disdain. This is how he had managed to construct his village, and one could already hear the rustling of his demonic motive for gathering these beings driven by their very nature toward wedlock with darkness. As the waters widened, they flowed along forested archipelagos. There were moments when the past reappeared, and Niklas once again saw the girl he'd known as he slept in Tartare's palace; he realized that the past, or what he believed to have happened, only existed as impossible memories from a life he hadn't lived, one to which he'd only aspired in his dreams.

Niklas's journal continues: *I have seen the demons of botany, of the most esoteric and disordered research, of libraries aflame, but by Saturn and its moons! No natural history had ever prepared me for demons that were so soft, with such exquisite skin . . . and Hoichi had witnessed things I'd only heard about in flawed, thirdhand versions: hordes of rats with reddened eyes out hunting, wearing the skins of animals they have killed, driving humans before them, using art beyond language to communicate, to organize the massive attacks. These rodents ambushed the*

humans perfectly, have abandoned the slum of darkness and now
rise up merciless, implacable, the voice of their hordes joined to
those of legion warrior beings.

According to Hoichi, still to come was the massive migra-
tion that would completely reconfigure the crust of the earth
for humans and nonhumans alike. It would be the biggest
mobilization of humanity since the Jews left Egypt, as if the
slow hordes crossing the Pacific to take possession of the
South American coastlines had sharply multiplied thousands
of times over. Hoichi's plan had been masterful, fully worthy
of an animal Head of State facing a flood: for three consecu-
tive years, the Portuguese clergy would proclaim throughout
the kingdom that mass emigration to Brazil was God's will.
They would emphasize the importance of bolstering the
Catholic faith in the region to confront the Protestant threat:
the prospect of annihilating an evil, unholy enemy would
encourage the most timid and excite the most fearful. The
Portuguese population would be transported en masse to
Brazil, and the territory of Portugal would be given to Spain,
whose empire would spread across the European continent.
Meanwhile, another empire of extraordinary grandeur and
unprecedented size would form in the New World, where
everything would be placed beneath the scepter of the house
of Bragança. The New World would devour the fundamental
lessons of the Old, and in the end would be master over it.
The hordes of Hoichi the Dark would cross the Black Atlantic
on a bridge made of all the dead slaves who lay piled at the
bottom of the ocean, would build their capital on the bank of
the world's largest river.

However, a species that can only relate to itself will over time create monstrosities that could lead to its extinction. It was thus imperative to enhance the relevant sexual behaviors so that lubricious desires could regain the path of protecting and exalting the desired form of the human project.

But as I stood there at the border of the precipice prepared for me, these faun women with their heads hanging down toward the earth, suspended in hammocks that the breeze hardly moved, a garden designed to propagate their insensate species, I had the premonition that within the dazzling light of the armored moon there was the tint of one prurient, evil ray: that here in this place I could easily be made one of those who breathe without seeing, could be added to his ring of corollas, could become another soldier in this motionless platoon of delicious parts. With only that thought in mind I let myself fall into what some must have perceived as unconsciousness, though in truth I had simply relinquished my powers. One of the women looked at me without speaking, and guided me to a small European-style greenhouse of iron and glass. I told them my name and looked around me. There was a map of the region showing which tribe had seized power in a given zone, which tribes were currently at war, which ate members of other tribes, and which territories belonged to beings who had never resigned their divine status and even now cut through the jungle like ferocious beasts. In the center of the map was the only thing that still commanded the respect of all involved: the great divide, the river, mesmerizing, deadly, serpentine.

The rat had been a member of one of the first squadrons formed in the darkness of the jungle. The Portuguese, expert travelers, had established amorous relationships with both their slaves and the natives, and whenever they resorted to torture, their hearts forced their eyes to close; their chests ached even as they raised the whip. The two elements that united them all were love and the jungle—the abundance of paradise.

Niklas and Tartare saw that the rat possessed several characteristics that were, in a veiled way, human. And in the smoothness of his long-fingered hands, in his refined manners, in the light gesture with which he gracefully thanked a servant, there was something distinctly feminine. He liked to wander the depths of the crater until he was no longer sure where he was; it reminded him of his early days here, when he swayed in the soft foliage and let his dreams lead him through the shiny slabs of mica that surged up through the soil like diamonds.

"Of course, for Portugal, submitting to Brazil was a logical impossibility, much as it was for Brazil to continue submitting to Portugal," he said philosophically, with the air of one who has taught himself to resemble his new brethren.

They didn't really know who he was; they referred to him as the Japanese man. The jungle closed in above me each time I tried to focus on him, to keep his outlines clear with the inner eye of my soul. I returned to wandering along the river, like part of a spell in which the most intimate material of my self was colluding with that being. Thinking about that bond, I felt myself collapse. At that moment he stretched out his arm, and I saw his gaunt hands clearly, a sickly pink shade. He gestured toward the jungle, the estuary, the boat, the river. His horrible rat teeth shone as he spoke, sealing his pact with the face of darkness under his command. I then thought that his life as a rat was only an instrument, a way to show us, like an emissary of light, the hidden evil, the death that stalks us, the shadows of the human heart.

I knew in that instant that I was going to work for him. There was no other way to remain here, and the rat promised survival.

The sun sweeps over all beings with a ruthless ferocity, and they hide from its terrifying gaze, because they know it to be a killer of creatures and men.

As for the rat himself, according to the story he told, he'd arrived in Rio de Janeiro just a few years before the Emperor moved his residence there from Lisbon; in short order, Hoichi had built his own small empire. Fascinated by the species in the area, he had established himself with the idea of studying them; soon, however, his home was destroyed by thugs who'd been organized as a force of order by some local inhabitants. There was nothing left in his house when he arrived: not his gowns, not the precious lenses he had hoped to mount in his laboratory, the magnifying glasses and other instruments that were so rare in this part of the world. Hoichi the Rat had to re-arm, but didn't know exactly how; he was a student of nature, and the interpersonal relationships that commerce demanded of him were hardly his strong suit. He went out walking, hoping for a providential idea. Perhaps Rio de Janeiro found his presence loathsome, but how to know for sure if he'd barely had a sniff around? He let himself wander down the streets that led to the beach, then followed a line of stele-like trees up to the bluffs. He laid down to rest beside a stream; it wasn't long before hunger and desperation closed in on him, and not a single idea had alighted upon him.

Returning to the jungle, he slept for weeks. In the course of his deep slumber, he wandered through areas whose existence he'd never even inferred: places where nature grows dense underground. He found a sort of labyrinth beneath the trees, the vestiges of a structure that dated back centuries, eaten away by rain, the jungle, and the rats. The discovery felt predestined, as if he'd spent his whole life moving forward between the light and the darkness of his existence for the sole purpose of descending into the hidden crater—as if burying himself in its depths would make him master of this inverted cathedral, where a god of catastrophe, an enemy of Heaven, might dedicate himself to delirium.

And then he saw them. A group of native women, each one a Venus of the stream. They were combing their hair in the water, and their audacity was so joyful, so completely lacking any form of discipline, that they seemed less like women than some species of local plant. It wasn't difficult to convince them to spend several days each week in the depths of his palace, drawn there by the allure of his *Crissia pallida* potions. Other women came—exquisite women with excellent dispositions, including Venetia d'Adda—and spent long afternoons conversing about modified species. For any man arriving for the first time, the sight was unheard-of: the women lay in hammocks in the dim light, completely naked and open like flowers. Most of them had lost consciousness, were submerged in a pleasurable stupor that lasted for several days. The men could go in and out as they pleased. In the anteroom, they could admire the orchids—*Zygopetalum*, *Noctilia pubescens*, *Bulbophyllum dentata*, *Brassavolas virginalis*, *Maxillarias draconii*. Technically, it wasn't even a brothel; Hoichi referred to it as a garden, a laboratory. He allowed the men's juices to accumulate inside each woman, then personally inserted pollinia, and gelatinous substances taken from the orchidian anatomy. He let them repose long enough for fecundation to take place, then extracted the altered juices together with the orgasmic fluids of the women. In a concrete sense, the women's bodies were themselves the laboratories, and he observed the behavior of the insects involved, researching, in a way, the mystery of mimesis.

Tartare understood immediately that I had to remain here in this place. I never saw him again. I still think about the woman, Lou, my Cerberus at the gates of darkness, whom I once saw disappear from the house of Tartare d'Hunval. Here I found her, and my body seemed to hurtle forward, transformed into electricity . . . and I thought, I should stop writing, I should linger here above her.

With Hoichi as host, the garden became a salon, a favorite gathering place among libertine scientists. It's clear that this is where Niklas got to know Lou; she often spent whole weeks naked and open, flowerlike. But Niklas was not content with the "slight contrasts within the human world at that time, the maelstrom of humors and vanities." He went to live in an austere house amongst the trees, and couldn't tolerate the company of anyone but women; he hired female servants so as to be surrounded by their aroma at all times. They agreed readily to his demand that they not bathe; from his writings, it's unclear whether or not he entered into sexual contact with them. He visited the garden obsessively, did research for Hoichi, no longer referred to him as "the rat." He stuck his tongue into a *Bulbophyllum*, and his tongue went numb for several hours. The underwater labyrinth of the mangrove swamps, and the coral formations that continue that labyrinth out below the obsidian mirror that separates human lives from those of the undersea world: all of this is present as illusion in his friend's salon.

All (the flowers) display themselves, and they emit something, something extra, an ether, the equivalent of the ether of past centuries, but this does not explain their movements. The orchids appear to have the ideal form, in the sense that there is no limit to the form they can take. How do species go about distinguishing the signals from the spectral noise of the jungle? We too must name the space in which emissions take place. Here the foliage grows thick and anything can happen.

The delicate balance that his mind required was lost: Niklas began to obsess over the nocturnal visits of hybrid beings. He no longer made cameo appearances in the diaries of others, no longer filled piles and piles of journals—or if he did, he left them somewhere safe from the eyes of the future. The idea of contemplating hybrid beings close up was so powerful that it soon consumed the rest of his research. He came to believe that he'd spent his whole life doing nothing but wading along the outer edges of the areas that surround the most exquisite, the most hidden of natural truths. Before leaving, he ran his fingers across Hoichi's, and then across Lou's, but she was lost in the vapors of *Crissia pallida*.

Max set his roller-ball pen down beside his notebook. Back in the early years of the company, he hadn't slept much. Now he had to take pills to sleep at all. He stayed motionless for a few seconds; he was facing a crucial moment in his research, in his life. He had finally found the formulation he'd been searching for, but it signified an incipient numbness, one that could last months, or years. He knew all too well the abstinence syndrome that afflicted his brain whenever his environment was anything but demanding, life-threatening. It wouldn't overtake him all at once, and he would be able to analyze each phase as it came; he would still be capable of aggregating certain functionalities, addressing certain complexities, entertaining himself by angering massive groups of people. But the work itself was done.

History is the history of symbiosis.

Human history is the history of the organisms and bacteria that inhabit us. The human phase of history's trajectory—its mendacity and its ethos—is a simplification that can be defined in epigenetic terms without denying the existence of ethical acts performed across the historical surface of the facts.

Max had a few buyers lined up—a sufficient number to create a bidding war behind closed doors. He was waiting for a text message from his preferred bidder, Markus Lenz, who managed a Chinese holding company specializing in big data, with substantial technological investments in Brazil. Max was about to get into the sauna when the message came through.

He hadn't said anything to his colleagues, except for Riccardo, who was the only one who knew that Stromatoliton was up for sale. Max turned off the sauna, sat back in his armchair, ate a few almonds. Stromatoliton, processor of the traces of beings, eye/brain machine that recreated the natural world's entire memory in a single location, would, in forty-eight hours, cease to belong to him.

Cassio bit his lip, tense with excitement. He knew that this was the equivalent of suicide, that he was destroying something beautiful, something he had helped to create; the taste of betrayal intensified his sensations. He grabbed a piece of paper and wrote:

I've seen things you people wouldn't believe.
C-beams
glitter
dark. Time to die.

He left the scrap of paper in front of Max Lambard's computer, knowing that its camera was present, framing the text for future reference. He had always been careful not to look at any camera directly, as doing so triggered the feedback parameters of algorithms designed to locate one's eyes, to track the passage of the gaze across the crust of things. Now he lifted his face, smiled without showing his teeth.

Hours earlier, he'd sent an encrypted message to Phillipe, in France, and to JP, at some undisclosed alpine location, one that, given the time of year of the endless winter sports season, would be somewhere up north—Whistler, maybe Banff. At eight P.M. EST, they would be awaiting his signal. With JP's help, Cassio had accessed a few hundred thousand computers distributed throughout the world, and had used them to launch an attack on several hundred thousand more potential victims. He'd installed a group of encrypted autonomous agents on each of the computers he'd hacked—the staggered process took much less time than he'd imagined. Each agent contained a line of code that would be triggered by the presence of a different set of stimuli; each set was unique, the result of a nontrivial compilation process that only the handful of academics who'd read his unpublished, undefended thesis would be in a position to understand, and even they wouldn't be able to decode it. *No one would suspect that the origin of the key governing the system was biological.* Together, the agents would function as a distributed database, where the keys needed to access all of the information collected by Stromatoliton remained latent; anyone could make use of them, but they couldn't be erased or modified. An algorithm within the encrypted code would connect the agents to the control libraries for each known quantum computer prototype: this is how the agents would distribute the constellations of data collected by Stromatoliton. Cassio's dark army had entered a new life. The agents would program each computer they accessed to seek out new traces with which to feed the database, thus weaving Stromatoliton's power into the very texture of the web. Access to the human trajectories Stromatoliton recorded would no longer depend on the viability of any given site; so long as the agents kept reproducing and the web retained computing power, Stromatoliton itself would continue to exist, but would reside beyond the reach of any given entity, including the state. And its behavior would remain encrypted, such that no one could know exactly what it was doing or where its parts were located; a mantle of opacity would spread out over the hostage data.

At the same time, imbedded in each agent was the portal's veiled nucleus. His beautiful fractal virus would stretch out its extremities and make contact with millions of bots. So long as a single agent continued to function, the entire infrastructure could be rebuilt, and access to Stromatoliton's results would remain public. No one could end the attack without destroying every single agent *at exactly the same time.*

It was Cassio's final heroic act as a hacker; in fact, it would be his final visible action, after which he would disappear forever into the jungle of anonymity. He thought about writing or calling Max, explaining the reasons for his betrayal, but each time he considered it, Max appeared in his mind to affirm that in the world of technology, betrayal is a contradiction *in adjecto.* Technology itself is a form of betrayal, forsaking its own nature in order to become something else. And this time, the very ability to disappear was at stake.

He left at dawn, carrying only his little backpack. He walked up the flagstone path without touching the grass. He crossed the empty parking lot, and the distant guard waved. The dancing ghosts of his breath froze in the air around his face, but he wasn't cold. On the contrary: he felt a constant inner boil, the result of either his excitation or his undiminished fever.

He walked directly to the first Bionose along his path, one on Bustillo Avenue, in front of the alpine rescue station. To a civilian, it would look no different from a regular security camera. He climbed up to it, knowing that in doing so he would attract attention, and also that his movements would be unintelligible. When he was right up next to the little holes, he blew a breath loaded with his genetic material. And the infection—the community to come—began to grow.

The virus wasn't discovered until several days after the company had been sold. By the time the money transfers were complete, it had been disseminated to each of the world's main botnets—the distributors of real content. Secure contracts in the blockchain made sure that the incentives were kept in check by a distributed army of willing ledger holders. When it reached a given computer, the virus created for them a crypto wallet; a few lines of code alerted the user to its own viral presence, adding that accepting the infection would give the user access to the data of the Stromatoliton universe. A lattice of secret trustholders and agents of mischief would form the collective self of the culprit. The cryptocurrency meant infection, which meant money: hence the incentives were aligned.

Cassio would not go down in history as a doer of any type; in fact, he wouldn't go down in history at all. Only the elite hacking circles would learn of Angzt's final blow, though his old time nickname was never typed in anywhere to be found.

Rumors about Stromatoliton's situation soon began to spread. The main one: that the maneuver sabotaging the recently sold company had taken place at the highest levels, which pointed to Max Lambard as its most likely author. When questioned by the press, Max worked actively to clarify the situation—he was still a shareholder in Stromatoliton, after all, albeit a minority one. He maintained a coherent, cooperative discourse with the ongoing investigation, explaining that the distribution attack had used keys that were encrypted years before, keys to which he never could have had access given that he wasn't the one who'd programmed them in the first place. Finding a private encryption key amidst the chaos of the world—"the preterite chaos which we have committed ourselves to organizing and making useful for everyone, a commitment to which we will remain dedicated through successive waves of technology"—was like looking for a needle across a manifold haystack of haystacks, when all of the haystacks except one held a plausible but inaccurate version of said needle. "At the moment, the computing power necessary to find the one true hash is unavailable," Max had said, smiling but stripped of all smugness.

Within a few weeks, the shadows of guilt had dissipated around him, and in time the charges were dropped. The act of democratizing the data had stripped away the value of the company he'd just sold, sending its share price into a dramatic dive. On the other hand, it was impossible to trace any action against the interests of the company back to him.

All such actions had been caught on film, and the company promised that it would deal internally with those responsible. When Max was given those tapes, he didn't care to play them. He'd seen them already, as they were taking place; he'd thought of sending Cassio surveillance footage, with the label "something to play at the wedding," but Cassio's location was untraceable, or at least Cassio thought he was, deep in the dark, becoming everything that moved, the beginning of an end and the end of something too. He saved it. Perhaps one day he'd post it online, in the middle of the ocean Web, like a song of baby whales who grew up together and recognize their voices. The world was so small, even if shattered. He knew where to find him.

Already on the mountain path, Cassio sent a text to Piera. He wanted to revel in his heroic sabotage, to tell her about the epic ideals he had never truly renounced. They had birthed the disaster together, and by now news of it would have reached circles that included Max Lambard. But Cassio couldn't say all these things, not in a text. Via darknet he sent her a picture of Cuento del Mar, a seafood restaurant in Puerto Montt that looked out over the Pacific. And if he ever saw her again—Cassio hoped that was still a possibility—he was thinking about proposing that they work together, maybe build their own laboratory.

By the time he learned that the company had changed hands, Cassio had already made his way over Cardenal Samoré Pass. At the customs office there, he'd been sniffed by a Chilean Bionose. He'd closed his eyes, concentrating on the sensation of floating out beyond the reach of all authority, on transmissions unimagined by earthly powers, but felt nothing out of the ordinary. He'd taken a deep breath and walked on.

The story of the epic but uneven battle between Cassio and Max, of clashing egos and monstrous betrayal, would dissolve into underground history within a few weeks. The virus, meanwhile, intersected with a substantial reservoir of advantageous DNA located in Jinquan, a prefect in the Gobi Desert. A prolific provider of DNA analysis to hospitals and laboratories worldwide, the Jinquan facility led the market for outsourced sequencing services. They were able to handle countless queries at once, and could provide any desired correlation from among the human avatars they had processed over the past decade, including some particularly fascinating mutation indices. Their decision to accept outsourced work had yielded unexpected fruit: they now possessed the world's largest genetic database, first and last names included. The only factor their clients cared about was price. When asked about the potential risks involved with handling such data and their strategy of using outsource contracts to increase volume, one company official commented that there was nothing to fear, that it was "best to think of us as inoffensive migrant workers" doing underpaid work—their triumph was so complete that they had the luxury of irony.

Cassio's virus found the perfect host there in Jinquan. It had been programmed simply to seek computational nodes that would enable it to grow ever stronger; while not implausible, it would have been difficult to foresee that in the course of its unfolding, the virus would happen across the world's richest source of genetic data. This final infection completed the protocols necessary to match genetic information to personal trajectory. The two multitudes—one living publicly on the surface of the skin, the other privately inside human organs—finally merged. The monster had reached its final phase.

And it went all but unnoticed. Cassio's strategy for distributing Stromatoliton's capabilities was so perfectly designed that open access to Jinquan's data reduced the value of the information it generated only momentarily. The world's stock markets, controlled by algorithms built for high-frequency trade, took just a few microseconds to relativize, to recommodify, to make the necessary adjustments. The market collapse was shocking, but lasted only a fraction of a millisecond; in that tiny lapse, a substantial amount of money changed hands so that everything else could stay exactly the same. A war had erupted inside the economic machine, and nothing had changed.

Outside, a meteorite shower was shattering the sky.

The emergence of new castes of beings is a common thread throughout the transformations. The process entails successive metamorphoses: primordial peoples traverse various modes of existence before reaching their current form. Along the way, bodies are built and unbuilt, with extreme permutations involving inter-specific corporeal forms. These forms often incorporate artifacts and body parts that were once corporeal forms in their own right. The conversions involved therein imply technological acts on the part of demiurgical creators.